MURDER

IN AN IRISH BOG

Police dig deep to solve a mystery

DAVID PEARSON

Paperback edition published by

The Book Folks

London, 2021

© David Pearson

ISBN 978-1-913516-88-8

www.thebookfolks.com

To David

Prologue

He reached out from his bed, waving his hand around near the floor, until it encountered the vodka bottle. He felt awful. He had drunk quite a measure of the stuff earlier, mixed with Coke from a one-litre plastic bottle that stood, uncapped, on the bedside locker. He poured the clear liquor into the earthenware mug he had been drinking from till it was a third full, and then topped it off with Coke, which by now had gone flat. He drank greedily, hoping that whatever was ailing him would be quelled by the mixture, and allow him to get off to sleep. But it was not to be.

His heart was beating faster now, and those agonising cramps in his stomach just would not go away. He tossed and turned, trying to get some degree of comfort for what seemed like an age.

Eventually, peace descended on him, and he finally lay quietly in the bed, although what he didn't know was that his major organs were failing. By morning he was stone cold dead.

A large plastic sheet was laid out beside the man, and he was rolled from the bed onto it. The plastic was then wound around the body and secured tightly with stout string all down its length. Then, the corpse was dragged and manhandled outside and into the waiting vehicle. It wasn't easy to do single-handedly, but after a lot of struggling, the body was pushed inside.

The vehicle set off in a puff of blue smoke. It bounced over the uneven ground for several miles, before coming to rest in a remote location where torrents of recent rainwater made rivulets and streams coming down from the mountain above, on their way to the lake below. The body was heaved out and dumped in the flow of the largest stream where the water immediately diverted around the obstacle to find another course down the incline and into the lake.

Chapter One

Sergeant Séan Mulholland arrived at Clifden Garda station at just after eight o'clock. It was a lovely bright September morning. The light had already changed from the hazy summer sunshine to the crisper autumnal hues, but there were no clouds to be seen in the clear blue sky as he pulled his ageing Saab up to the front of the station; it was noticeably cooler than it had been just a couple of weeks previously.

Mulholland was approaching sixty years of age, and could have retired some years ago from the force. But he was a bachelor, and was identified by his position in charge of the Garda station in Clifden, and in any case, what would he do, stuck in his rather dilapidated cottage out on the Sky Road if he didn't have work to go to? He enjoyed the socializing that went with the job, and the certain amount of status that it afforded him in the community.

Once inside the single storey building, Mulholland left his peaked cap on the front counter to indicate that there was an official presence in the station and made his way to the back of the premises where a small kitchenette was located. He filled the electric kettle and put it on to boil for his first cup of tea of the day – a well-rehearsed ritual that he always performed first thing.

The postman didn't arrive until much later in the day, so in the early hours the sergeant could catch up on a few emails and read some of the electronic bulletins that had come out from the Regional Headquarters in Galway, or even from the Phoenix Park itself, which was the location for the overall management of the police force in Ireland.

He prepared his tea, and took it through to the main office – an area separated from the front office, which was open to the public, by a screen made of wood from the waist down, and frosted glass in the upper section, so that those in the middle office could see if anyone came into the station.

By nine o'clock Jim Dolan and Séamus Gill had arrived, followed by the rest of the eleven staff that made up the strength of the Gardaí in this normally quiet Connemara town. When the station had filled up, Mulholland announced that he was going for a stroll to see if there was anything going on round and about.

Clifden was quiet at this time of year, the main cohort of tourists having retreated back to their own homes now that the schools had returned for the autumn term. Nearly all of the lock-up-and-leave properties, busy with the good citizens of Galway and even Dublin during the months of high summer, were closed for the winter, their owners hoping that the ravages of the prevailing south-westerly winds would not be too hard on their holiday homes until they could return at Easter the following year.

Mulholland left the station and turned towards the town centre. He walked past the new Aldi supermarket, on past the old schoolhouse and was soon passing Ferris's petrol station that was just opening up. The establishment had four pumps – two for petrol, one for diesel and another for farm diesel which was sold for agricultural machinery at a reduced rate of tax. Ferris had a shop of sorts too, where basic provisions such as bread, milk, eggs, tea and coffee could be purchased along with a wide variety of snacks and even whipped ice cream cones in the summer months.

Mulholland turned up the steep incline of Main Street and bid good day to the proprietors of the various shops that were preparing their businesses for what would, in all probability, be another quiet day of trade – at least until the afternoon when the children were released from school and their mothers brought them into town to make some modest purchases.

Feeling a little out of breath as he approached Foyle's Hotel, he decided to go into the post office next door to see how his old friend Bridget O'Toole was doing. Both Mulholland and O'Toole had put in nearly seventy years of service between them, looking after the citizens of Clifden. Mulholland dispensed justice, while O'Toole dispensed allowances and benefits as well as stamps, postal orders and a good deal of free advice to all who frequented the little premises.

The bell attached to the top of the post office door tinkled as Mulholland entered, and a moment later Bridget appeared from the back of the shop.

"Ah, 'tis yourself, Séan. Grand morning, isn't it?" Bridget said.

"God, it is. It'll be like this for the month now, I imagine."

"Let's hope so. Maybe it will bring a few more tourists to the town, though we haven't had a bad year all round. How has it been for you, Séan?"

"Fairly busy now, to be honest. We've had a good few smartarses out from the city. They think they can do what they like once they get beyond Recess. But thankfully, nothing too serious."

"God, I'm forgetting my manners. Would you like a cup of tea, Séan?"

"Ah, no thanks, Bridget. I'm just after having one down at the station. So, is there any news?"

Séan Mulholland ran the Clifden Garda station, in as much as it was possible these days, in the old style. He believed strongly in community policing, and was well respected in the vicinity, so that if there was anything untoward going down, he would usually pick it up from the locals, and Bridget O'Toole was always one of the best informed.

"No, I don't think so. But wait a minute, have you heard anything about Davin Faherty recently?"

"No, nothing. Why do you ask?"

"Well, he's always in here bright and early of a Friday to collect his dole money. He might miss a week sometimes when he's working away in the city, or up in Westport, but he never lets it go this long. I haven't seen him for four weeks now – it will be five on Friday if he doesn't turn up."

"What about his brother – Laughlin, is it?"

"Yes, that's the brother's name, but we never see him in here. He must get his money sent directly to the bank."

"Do you think there's something wrong, Bridget?"

"Well now, Séan, that's your department. But it's not normal, is all I'll say."

"Righto. I'll get one of the lads to call out to the farm later on and see what the story is. They live out in Boolagare if I remember rightly," Mulholland said.

"Yes, although I'd hardly call it a farm. But that's where they're from, all right."

"Fair enough. Well, I'll leave you in peace now Bridget. I'll let you know how we get on with the Fahertys."

"Thanks, Séan. It will just put my mind to rest."

After Mulholland had left the shop, turned left at the top of the street and walked back down Market Street, he started to think.

"That's a bit odd, all right. Maybe I'll go out with Jim and see what's what, later on."

Chapter Two

Boolagare is a township that lies inland from the sea near Ballyconneely. It had originally been part of the barony of Ballynahinch, but the land was so poor that it had been given over to common ownership in the nineteenth century by the then owner Valentine Blake, who, by this means avoided having to pay rates on what was essentially worthless scrub. Made up of approximately 550 acres of bog, interspersed with massive limestone boulders, the land was more or less incapable of supporting any kind of agricultural endeavour. The name, translated from Irish, means Short Dairy, although if there ever was a dairy in the location, it was long since abandoned.

There were a small number of dwellings in the townland which dated back to the mid-nineteenth century when famine ravaged much of Ireland, and the Faherty brothers occupied one of these.

The property was constructed of stone – of which there was an abundance in the area – covered in wattle and daub composed of straw, peat and animal dung, and then, when dry, painted over with whitewash. The floor was originally clay, but the brothers' father had flagged it out in the 1960s, when some other improvements were made to the house, including the installation of electricity.

More recently, the brothers, who never got on – even when they were children – had subdivided the property, so that Davin occupied the two rooms to the left of the entrance, one leading off the other, while Laughlin took the rooms on the right. The kitchen occupied the central section of the property and the bathroom – such as it was – was shared, being situated behind the kitchen. But the two lads had arranged cooking times so that they didn't have to meet at mealtimes, such was the acrimony between them.

Laughlin, being the more industrious of the two brothers by some measure, had modernised his part of the accommodation, so that it was clean and cosy and even quite tastefully furnished. Davin's quarters, by contrast, were dirty and dowdy as he had made little change to the place since his parents died some eight years previously, leaving the whole house to be shared between the brothers; although in time-honoured style, Laughlin, as the elder of the two, officially held the title to the place. To the left-hand side of the cottage stood a large shed with a rusting corrugated iron roof which housed some bits of ancient machinery, and could be used, at a push, to keep the cattle out of the weather if it turned very bad.

Laughlin had always been the more industrious of the two boys. When he was just seventeen he embarked upon a scheme to remove the huge stones from several acres of the land which the Fahertys grazed, and put in drainage. The result was that he could keep a few bullocks over the summer months and fatten them for the factory where they were sent each autumn, supplementing the meagre income that otherwise relied on sheep. Further endeavours from the young man saw another few acres turned over to grassland which produced hay in the early summer and grazing for the cattle for the rest of the season, as long as there was growth on the land. But it was hard work. Too hard for Davin who thought his brother a fool to be slogging it out in the fields, especially when the weather was inclement. Davin preferred working indoors, and occupied himself painting and decorating, and doing a bit of light building work when the humour took him. But a lot of the time he was idle, and that, Laughlin thought, was his brother's natural state.

* * *

When Sergeant Mulholland got back to the Garda station it was after eleven o'clock, and Paddy the postman had been leaving several items that required the signature of the Member in Charge. Mulholland asked Séamus Gill if there was anything else going on that he should be aware of, and Gill filled him in on a call they had received at around ten o'clock.

"We had a call from a Mrs Sweeney out at Mannin. She thought she saw someone snooping around one of the holiday homes last night, and she said there may have been a light on in the house later on," Gill said.

"Fat lot of use telling us now then, don't you think?"

"Ah well, she probably didn't want to make a fuss. Anyway, Jim has gone out to have a look just in case, but I'd say it's nothing. We haven't had any trouble out that way recently."

"You'd better give Jim a call and see if he needs any help. I'll be in the office looking after this lot," Mulholland said, waving the fistful of documents in the air as he departed.

"Fine. I'll give him a shout."

Jim Dolan had walked all around the bungalow, positioned opposite the wide, sandy beach at Mannin, a couple of hundred metres further on than Mrs Sweeney's house. Finding nothing amiss, he called to the woman to see if she had anything to add, but found that there was no more to report.

"We'll give the owner a call later and see if he can shed any light on it. But don't you worry, Mrs Sweeney. If you see anything like that again, call us straight away and we'll come out at once."

Having enjoyed Mrs Sweeney's hospitality which ran to two cups of tea and some excellent home-made soda bread and jam, Dolan made his way back to the Garda station.

* * *

"Ah, Jim, there you are," Mulholland said when Dolan came back in. "Was there anything going on out in Mannin to concern us?"

"I don't think so. I'll give the owner of the house a call and see if he can tell us anything, but the place looked secure enough – no sign of any interference in any case."

"Fair enough. Oh, by the way, I'd like you and I to go out to Faherty's up at Boolagare early tomorrow. Bridget in the post office says she hasn't seen young Davin for a few weeks, and that's unusual. Can you pick me up at eight o'clock tomorrow and we'll get out there before Laughlin disappears off across the bog for the day?"

"Yes, of course. I'll tell Séamus he's on opening up duties."

* * *

The weather was holding up well the following morning when Jim Dolan stopped outside Séan Mulholland's bungalow at the appointed hour.

"God, the man would want to put a few bob into this place before it gets any worse," he said to himself, regarding the faded paintwork, dirty windows with decrepit net curtains hanging down inside, and copious weeds sprouting up through the thin gravel on the driveway.

He was just getting out of the car to ring the doorbell when Mulholland appeared.

"Good morning, Sarge. Another lovely day," Dolan said.

"Morning, Jim. It is indeed."

Despite the downtrodden appearance of Mulholland's bungalow, Dolan had to admit that the location was spectacular. It had an uninterrupted view to the coast and out to sea, and the evening views of the sun going down over the Atlantic Ocean must be breath-taking, he thought.

The two men set off in Dolan's car in the early morning sunshine.

"Do you know where we are headed?" Mulholland asked.

"Boolagare, isn't it? Where those two Faherty brothers live."

"Yes, that's it. I was looking them up on our system last evening before I left the station. Young Davin has a few minor offences logged – you know, driving without insurance or tax, drunk and disorderly and a bit of shoplifting from when he was much younger. But Laughlin has a clean sheet. Nothing at all."

"That's often the way. The younger ones are usually the troublemakers – especially boys. But he doesn't exactly sound like a master criminal all the same."

"No, I agree – but they're only the things he was caught for. God knows what else he's been up to."

The two men drove on in that easy silence that often exists between male work colleagues who have known each other for a long time. There was nothing to be said in any case, until they turned off the main R341 just past Ballyconneely onto the unmarked road that led to Boolagare.

"What exactly are we looking for here, Sarge?" Dolan said.

"I just want to check out where Davin might be. He hasn't been seen around the town for a while, and Bridget

O'Toole says that's very unusual. It's probably nothing, but let's see what his brother has to say."

"Fair enough. God, this boreen goes on forever."

After another mile or thereabouts bouncing over the steadily deteriorating track which now had weeds and grass growing up in the centre, they arrived at the homestead. Dolan turned the car in through the rusty iron gate, and brought it to rest on the wide expanse of cracked concrete in front of the cottage.

The two men got out, and Mulholland went to the door of the house and knocked firmly twice. Dolan strolled over to the left of the dwelling and looked inside the large barn where an old red Ferguson tractor was parked. Further to the left, languishing in the tall grass and weeds was the remains of a black Morris Minor bearing what Dolan recognized as the old ZM County Galway registration from the 1960s. Greenery was growing up through the car, the front windscreen of which had been removed, but the back of the old machine was in remarkably good shape, with just a few rust bubbles showing along the lower edge of the boot door.

Laughlin Faherty opened the door.

"God, it's yourself, Sergeant. What brings you out this way on this fine September morning?"

"Hello, Laughlin. Sorry to bother you – can I come in?"

"Of course." Laughlin stood aside to usher Mulholland into the kitchen of the little house.

Mulholland removed his peaked cap, and at Laughlin's invitation sat down on a bare wooden chair beside the well-scrubbed kitchen table.

"Can I get you a cup of tea, Sergeant?"

"Ah, no, you're grand. We don't want to keep you from your work," Mulholland said.

Laughlin was dressed in denim dungarees with Wellington boots and a dark green knitted cardigan to keep out the early morning chill.

"We were just wondering about Davin. Is he around at all?" Mulholland said.

"No, thank God, he's not – idle so-and-so."

"Right. Do you know where he is, Laughlin?"

"What's he done now, Sergeant? He's good for nothing that lad."

"No, he hasn't done anything. We just need a word with him, if you could tell me where he is just now?"

"I can't say. But that's not unusual. He often disappears for a while, and to be honest, I haven't a clue where he ends up. We don't get on that well you know – never have."

"When did you last see him?"

"Oh, it must be a good few days – maybe even a week or two. I don't keep track of his movements."

"I see. And do you know if he has a mobile phone at all?"

"I think he has, but don't ask me for the number. I hate those things," Laughlin said.

"And tell me, Laughlin, what does he drive these days?"

"He had an old car a while back, but he had no insurance or tax, and Garda Brosnan caught him going through Roundstone one night with no lights on, and prosecuted him. He sold the old banger then – I think he gave it to Deasy for a hundred euro or so."

"So how does he get about? It's not exactly an easy place to get in and out of if you haven't got transport."

"Search me. Look, Sergeant, I have as little to do with my brother as possible. We're very different. Davin doesn't like hard work, and scrounges off anyone that he can. I've made something out of this patch of bog over the years, and I've managed to carve out a living where lots of folk would have said it wasn't possible, and I enjoy it. It's hard work, but very rewarding. But as for Davin, it wouldn't bother me if I never saw him again – honestly."

"I see. That's a shame, Laughlin. How long is it since your parents passed?"

Laughlin gave the sergeant a wry look.

"It's just about eight years since my father went. My mother died the year before, as I'm sure you know."

"And does Davin own half of this place?"

"He does. That's the only reason I put up with him at all. It was my father's dying wish that the place be split between us, even though Davin never contributed as much as a day's work to getting it right. But he was always the apple of my mother's eye – he could do no wrong, so that's the way it was left."

"I see. Well, Laughlin, if you do see him, maybe you'd ask him to get in touch with me in Clifden – maybe call in to the station. Before we go, would it be OK to have a look in his room?"

"If you want, but you may need protective clothing. It's pretty rough in there," Laughlin said with half a grin, nodding to the door that led to the younger brother's quarters.

Mulholland went to the door and summoned Jim Dolan. The two of them donned blue vinyl gloves, and went into the rooms that Davin occupied in the divided house. Laughlin hadn't been exaggerating. The first room – a sitting room of sorts – was very dirty and untidy with empty beer cans strewn around and a couple of rancid cushions parked on the sofa, which had definitely seen better days as it was sagging badly in the middle. There was little other furniture, save for an old television perched on a wooden side table and another old armchair that was in worse condition than the settee.

The two men pressed on into the bedroom. Here, a single bed with filthy sheets and an indescribable duvet sat against the wall. Discarded clothes were strewn about the floor, and an old wooden wardrobe stood with its mirrored door open, revealing a few jackets and pants hanging on misshapen metal coat hangers. A bedside locker contained a few paperbacks, and a small selection of medication including two sachets of Lemsip and a small tub of paracetamol tablets. Three pairs of filthy trainers and two pairs of worn socks under the bed completed the picture.

Dolan spent a moment rummaging through the drawer at the base of the wardrobe, but it yielded nothing but some more clothes in various stages of disrepair.

"Doesn't look like he emigrated, anyway," Dolan said, standing up again.

Mulholland and Dolan went back out to where Laughlin Faherty was tidying up the kitchen area.

"Well, thanks very much, Laughlin. We'll be off now. But tell me, are you not a bit worried at all that your brother seems to have disappeared?"

"No, Sergeant, I'm not. As I told you, if I never see him again it will be too soon!"

Chapter Three

Senior Inspector Maureen Lyons had been put in charge of the newly formed Serious and Organised Crime Unit as part of the Western Division of the Garda Síochána based in Galway City. The new arrangement was an experiment of sorts, embarked upon by senior management of the force in an effort to curtail the increase in criminal activity that was beginning to take hold in the region. But it was more than that. It was the first such unit to be established outside Dublin, and it was the first to be headed up by a female inspector, so there was a lot riding on its success.

Lyons had a lot of support. To begin with, her life partner was Detective Superintendent Mick Hays. The two of them had been living together for a number of years out in Salthill, and although the arrangement was a little irregular, it had worked well for them both, and for the force itself. Chief Superintendent Finbarr Plunkett, who had overall responsibility for the Gardaí in the area, had initially been sceptical about two of his senior officers being romantically attached, but he had seen how well things were working out to the benefit of all concerned, and had eventually admitted that there wasn't an issue.

Lyons had been given her pick of the available resources when the unit was established, and she had surrounded herself with a strong team. She had brought Peadar Tobin – previously a uniformed Garda from Clifden – into the city, and she had seconded Detective Sergeant Sally Fahy to the cause as well. Two other Detective Gardaí had been assigned – one each from Sligo and Limerick – providing a core of five officers, but she could also call on Inspector Eamon Flynn and others when there was a serious operation taking place.

The SOCU worked in a very different style to normal detecting. Usually, detectives responded to a crime immediately, knowing that in the case of murder for example, the trail could go cold very quickly if they weren't on the ball. It is often said that they had about two weeks to solve a serious crime, and after that the chances of bringing the perpetrator to book were greatly reduced.

With organised crime, detection worked differently. It was often a long and painstaking investigation, putting tiny pieces of a complex jigsaw together over many months, culminating in a major operation where a number of suspects were arrested at the same time, though frequently not in the same place. Co-ordination with other divisions within the force, and even outside agencies was required, and there were lots of opportunities to get things wrong or for some vital piece of the jigsaw to leak out to the criminals, giving them an opportunity to avoid capture.

Over the summer months, Lyons and her team had been working on such a case. Organised criminals had been stealing farm and building machinery, driving to a nearby town, and smashing ATM machines out of the walls of banks, supermarkets and petrol stations and making off with them. It was a sophisticated operation, requiring extensive planning and very rapid execution. The actual attack on the machines, which happened in the small hours, took as little as ten minutes all told, and in many cases, there was no CCTV or any other evidence to help identify the thieves.

Thanks to dogged detective work, information gleaned from a few snouts and quite a degree of luck, the Gardaí had received information on where such a heist was to take place. The gang duly arrived, and set about their task with determination and haste, hacking the ATM out from the brick wall in which it was located and tying canvas straps around it to load it onto the back of a half-cab truck using the same JCB that had been used to smash the wall.

While the thieves were busy – there was just five of them in all – the Gardaí had rolled a couple of eight-wheel sand lorries across the road, one in each direction of escape, and when the thieves drove off with the spoils of their endeavours without any lights on their truck, they promptly crashed into one of these obstacles and came to a shuddering halt.

Armed Response Unit officers were waiting, concealed near the sand lorries, and quickly descended on the absconders with their sub-machine guns raised. One of the gang was seen to reach into the glove box of the escape vehicle to retrieve a handgun, but a quick-witted ARU officer stuck the muzzle of an MP4 up against the man's face and calmly said, "Touch that, and I'll blow your brains out."

When Lyons saw that the situation was under control, she went to the driver's door of the half-cab and opened it.

"I'm just the driver. I ain't got nothing to do with this lot," squealed the young man who had gashed his forehead during the crash, and now had a small trickle of blood down his face.

"Right, and I'm fucking Cinderella," Lyons said, signalling to one of her uniformed colleagues to handcuff the man and read him his rights.

In a follow-up operation, the carcasses of two more stolen ATMs were found in a shed adjacent to the farm of the father of one of the gang, and €25,000 was also recovered that had been put into an empty animal feed bag and covered in straw.

It was in this manner that the Galway-based SOCU became established as a force to be reckoned with. Management in the Gardaí were suitably impressed with the performance, and made much of it in the media.

Lyons, in typical self-deprecating manner, told the inevitable press conference after the event was over, "We got lucky. But we want to send a message to anyone else who might be thinking of committing a similar crime in the west of Ireland – we're coming for you. You will be caught, and you will spend a lot of years in jail."

But in this business, the warm afterglow of success doesn't last long. There are always new challenges to be tackled.

* * *

Lyons was struggling through the extensive paperwork associated with the ATM thefts. There were statements and affidavits to be collated, bodycam footage to be gone through, not to mention literally masses of forensic evidence including fingerprints, shoe prints, DNA, all of which had to be sorted and catalogued in the correct order as part of the State's case against the five lads who had been apprehended at the scene.

Her phone rang.

"Hi, Maureen. It's Séan here. How's it going?"

"Ah, you know. More paperwork than I like, but it's OK, I guess. What about you?"

"God, that was a fair bit of work you did with those lads out on the Tuam Road. You'll be famous after that."

"It was a team effort, Séan, but yes, a good result all around. What's on your mind?" she said, keen to move the conversation on, but not wanting to be in any way short with the man. She had a lot of respect for Mulholland, even if some in the force thought he was a bit past it.

"It's probably something and nothing, but I wonder if you could make a few enquiries about a young fella by the name of Davin Faherty? He has a place out here at Boolagare with his brother, Laughlin, but he seems to have gone missing. I thought maybe he's gone into the city, and some of ye might be able to track him down."

"Has the brother reported him as a missing person, Séan?"

"No, not exactly. It was the woman in the post office who put me onto it. He hasn't collected his dole money for a few weeks, and she says that's very unusual. We went out to see the brother, and by the looks of it, the young fella hasn't packed up his stuff or anything, so I'm not sure what's going on – but it doesn't feel right."

"Have you a photograph of this bloke – what did you call him again?"

"Faherty. Davin Faherty. I haven't, but he's in the system from way back. You should be able to get a picture of him handy enough."

"OK, Séan, I'll put the word out and see what I can do. It's not something I'd normally deal with, but seeing as its you, I'll have a go at it."

"Ah, thanks, Maureen. It could be nothing, but I just have a feeling, if you know what I mean."

"I do. Give it a few days, and if you haven't heard anything, give me another call. Thanks, Séan."

* * *

Later that evening, Lyons was at home with Mick Hays. They were having a meal and a bottle of wine, and by way of conversation, Lyons relayed the details of the phone call she had had from Séan Mulholland.

"Boolagare, Boolagare, why does that place sound familiar to me?" Hays said.

"You've heard of it then?"

"I have, but I can't remember how or why. But it will come to me. What did you say the name was again?"

"Faherty. Two brothers apparently – Laughlin and Davin. Davin is the younger, and by all accounts they don't get on."

When they had finished the meal and cleared up, the two of them sat down in easy chairs in the lounge. Maureen turned on the TV, while Hays took out his laptop and started browsing.

"Boolagare – here you go. I knew I'd seen that name mentioned somewhere recently. It seems there's talk of an American mining company looking for exploration rights out that way. They've applied for a license for a large area including Boolagare and right across as far as Dog's Bay."

"God, you can't be serious. They can't start digging up that place – it would be a scandal. Where is the application at now?"

"It doesn't say, but there's talk of copper deposits and maybe even gold!"

"Bloody hell, Mick!"

"Yes, the place would be badly impacted, that's for sure. Even if the mining company behaved themselves, can you just imagine the number of amateur prospectors that would descend on the place. It would be chaos."

"Hmm. You've got me interested now. Tomorrow, I'm going to have a look, see if there's anything going on that we should know about. It's hardly connected to Davin Faherty – but you never know."

Chapter Four

When Lyons arrived in to work the following morning, she asked Sally Fahy to come into her office.

"Hi, Sally. I wonder if you could do something for me?"

"Sure, boss. What's up?"

Lyons told Fahy about the phone call she had had with Séan Mulholland the previous day.

"Could you put the word out amongst the uniformed Gardaí to keep an eye out for Davin Faherty? There's no need to bring him in if they find him, just let us know where he's living and what he's up to. Keep it very low key. He hasn't been officially reported as missing – well, not yet anyway."

"OK, sure. But isn't this a bit off the beaten track for us?"

"Yes, it is. But Séan is an old friend, and he's asked me for a favour, so let's just do it and not make a fuss. OK?"

"Yes, of course. No problem."

* * *

Séan Mulholland had a stone in his shoe. He was quite unsettled following the conversation with Laughlin

Faherty, and he couldn't just let it rest. He called Pascal Brosnan who ran the Garda station in Roundstone – a small fishing and tourist village half an hour from Clifden – together with another Garda, Mary Fallon by name.

"Good morning, Pascal. I wonder if you could do something for me this morning?"

"Hello, Sergeant. Yes of course. What do you need?"

"Could you go out as far as Deasy's garage, and see if he has had any dealings with a Davin Faherty of late. If he has, get the details for me."

"Righto, Sarge. What's this all about?" Brosnan asked.

"Ah, 'tis probably nothing, so just do as I ask and let me know, will you?"

"Yes, of course. I'll call you later."

Brosnan was puzzled about the phone call, but knew better than to question his boss. He told Mary that she was in charge, and he set off out to Deasy's garage which was located in a yard some three kilometres the other side of Roundstone on the road to Recess.

When he pulled into the rather dilapidated premises, Tadgh Deasy was there with his head stuck under the bonnet of an old Toyota van. He looked up when he heard Brosnan's car arrive, hoping that it might be a customer.

Brosnan got out of the car and walked over to where the garageman was working.

"Good morning, Tadgh. Do you think you'll ever get that thing going again?" Brosnan quipped, noticing that the tax disk in the windscreen of the van had expired some months ago.

"Of course I will. It's just in for a service. Plenty of miles left in the old thing yet. What can I do for you anyway, Pascal?"

"I was just wondering if you'd seen Davin Faherty recently – you know the lad that lives over at Boolagare?"

"Davin? God, that's a coincidence. I have. Wasn't he in here about three weeks ago?"

"I see. And what was his business with you, Tadgh?"

Deasy had some fence-mending to do with the Gardaí after they had found him messing around with Northern Ireland registration plates a few months back, so he was happy to tell Brosnan the details of the transaction that Faherty and himself had concluded.

"He brought in an old Opel Corsa. A bit of a wreck. It's still over there," Deasy said, nodding to a very sad-looking car with much of its red paint faded and peeling at the other side of the yard.

"He was looking for something a bit better to drive, so I took it in and sold him a nice little Golf I had here. It was a cracker. Belonged to a nurse who worked in Clifden, but she was emigrating, and wanted a quick sale. Only had 50,000 kilometres on the clock."

"And I'm sure you gave her a fair amount for it, Tadgh."

"Of course I did. And yer man was glad to get it."

"How much did that cost him?"

"I gave it to him at a rare good price – for a quick sale, you know. I have the details inside the house. C'mon in and I'll look it up for you."

The two men made their way across the yard to Deasy's house and went into the kitchen where Brosnan took a seat at the bare wooden table.

"Would you like a brew while you're here, Pascal?" Deasy said.

"Aye, right enough, that would be grand."

Deasy prepared a pot of strong tea, and managed to root out a packet of digestive biscuits to go with it, and he sat down with his new best friend.

"So, what about the Golf then?"

"Oh, right. I have the papers here in the drawer," Deasy said, getting up and going across to the large dresser that sat against the wall of the kitchen.

"Here we are. Faherty gave me €12,500 for the Golf – plus his own car. But I reckon it's only worth €50 for parts. It's a right jalopy. That reminds me, I must send in the change of ownership thing. That slipped my mind."

"And was that cash, Tadgh?"

"Yes, it was. All nice new notes too, wrapped and all with the bank brand on them."

"And you weren't a bit curious about where Davin Faherty would get such an amount in cash?" Brosnan said.

"None of my business. And anyway, why look a gift horse...?"

"Hmm... OK. Well, I need the registration number of the Golf," Brosnan said, taking out his notebook and copying the number from the registration book that Tadgh Deasy still had in his possession.

"And what colour is the VW, Tadgh?"

"Black. Great paint on her too. That nurse looked after it right well."

"So, did Faherty say anything about what he was doing at all?" Brosnan asked.

"No, he's not a very talkative soul at the best of times. But whatever he's up to he has a decent set of wheels under him now at least. Why, what's your interest, Pascal?"

"Ah, nothing much. He hasn't been seen anywhere for a few weeks, and the sergeant thinks it's a bit odd – that's all."

"Probably used his new motor to pull some lady from the city and is shacked up with her thinking all his birthdays have come at once!"

Brosnan smiled.

"Aye, you could be right. Anyway, I'd better get going. Look, if he comes in again, or if you see him or hear anything about him, give me a call, won't you? And don't forget to send in the change of ownership documents."

"Right so. I'll do that today. I have to go into Roundstone to get some stuff and I'll post it when I'm there. Thanks for reminding me, Pascal," Deasy said, without a hint of irony.

When Brosnan got back to the Garda station, he phoned Séan Mulholland to relay the conversation he had had with Tadgh Deasy.

"Do you think he was on the level, Pascal?"

"I do, Sergeant. He needs to keep straight with us after that business with the Northern Ireland plates. And I'd say he made a good killing on the Golf. Probably only paid the poor girl 5,000 euro for it and sold it to Faherty for more than double. Anyway, I told him to let us know if he sees or hears from Davin, so that's about all we can do."

* * *

It was a quiet evening in Mill Street Garda station, and Lyons, Fahy, Flynn and Tobin were sitting around having a cup of tea before they all headed home for the night.

By way of conversation, Lyons mentioned the chat she had had with Séan Mulholland about the missing Faherty brother.

"God, that's gas. My family used to have grazing rights up around Boolagare. My grandfather kept a few sheep round about, and he was always having to go out and collect them up – usually in the worst weather you can imagine. I used to give him a hand if I was there," Peadar Tobin said.

"Where did they live, Peadar?" Sally Fahy asked.

"They had a place near Maumeen Lough, just off the Ballyconneely Road. It wasn't much of a place, but my grandfather had it quite nice, and my father did a lot of work on it too."

"Is that where you grew up, Peadar?" Lyons asked.

"No. We had a smallholding up at Ballinaboy where at least you could grow a few crops, and do a bit of fishing. My father was a very industrious man. He worked all the hours at one thing or another, and we always had plenty and were well looked after. Then, when his father died, he kept the grazing at Boolagare as well, but it's fierce bad land."

"Did you know the Fahertys then?" Lyons went on.

"Kinda. Not well, but I knew who they were and we'd see them at mass in Clifden by times. They had it hard though. But Laughlin seems to have made something of the place."

When the tea had all been consumed, the detectives began to depart one after another, but Peadar Tobin remained behind. The talk of his old homeland had sparked an interest, and he sat down at one of the office computers and started searching on Google.

Chapter Five

The week went by without further incident. Sally Fahy had done as Lyons had asked, and had put the word out with the uniformed division of the force that they were keen to know the whereabouts of Davin Faherty. She had followed up on it a few days later, but there was no news, and she relayed this to Lyons.

"There's no sign of Davin Faherty, boss. But I did come across something else of interest."

"Oh, thanks, Sally. What's that then?"

"The uniformed lads think there may be a grow house set up out near the University. It's just something they heard when they were asking about Faherty. Do you think we should take a look?"

"Definitely. Do you have an address?"

"Not exactly, but allegedly it's in one of the small cottages out on the Newcastle Road just where it turns into St Mary's Road. You know, close to the junction where that chemist's shop is," Fahy said.

"OK. Let's go out and have a look. We'll go in yours. Less obvious."

"Do you not think we should alert the Drug Squad, boss?"

"Nah. Not yet anyways. If it turns out to be nothing we'd look right eejits."

* * *

Lyons and Fahy drove out to the area where they believed the grow house was located. They parked in front of the pharmacy, and Fahy went in to make a small purchase that she didn't need just to make it look genuine in case the place was being watched. The suspect house was adjoining a fast food outlet. The little cottage had two windows to the front, either side of a hall door, and they appeared to be shuttered from inside.

"Let's just take a stroll down along and see if we can see the rear of the premises, Sally."

They walked along St Mary's Road for a few metres, and from a gap in the houses they could just about get a glimpse of the back wall of the suspect house. They could see a small flue sticking out through a hole that had been roughly hacked out of the masonry, and there was steam or smoke issuing from it.

"That's a clever move, Sally. The vent from the take-away is right beside it, so it wouldn't arouse any curiosity. And the smell of the fried food would disguise the smell of the cannabis if that's what's actually going on."

"What do you want to do, boss?"

"Let's have a look around here for a bit. See what's what."

The two women walked down St Helen's Road for about a hundred metres and then turned and went back along the other side of the road. They then got back into Fahy's car, hoping that their snooping hadn't aroused any suspicion if someone was observing, but they could see no evidence of anyone taking any interest.

Back in the car, Fahy said, "What do you think we should do?"

"I'd like to set up an observation on the house. Those plants need to be tended regularly, and if I know anything, that will take place under cover of darkness. I think the house on the corner of St Helen's Street is empty. See if you can find out who owns it, and if we can gain access to mount surveillance."

"OK. Let's get back, and I'll see what I can do."

* * *

Back at the station, Fahy went off to see if she could track down the owner of the house on the corner of the Newcastle Road and St Helen's Road. Lyons went to her office, and a moment later, Peadar Tobin knocked on the door.

"Come in, Peadar. What's up?" Lyons said, indicating that he should take a seat.

"Ah, probably nothing. But after everyone went home the other night, I got onto Google and did some searching around about Boolagare – just for old times' sake. I came across an article in the Tribune that caught my attention. It seems that some American outfit is looking to do mining out there. They applied for a license to explore for copper and even gold in that whole area – right over as far as Dog's Bay."

"Yeah, Mick said something about that to me the other night. Did you ever hear about gold out that direction, Peadar?"

"No, I never did. But this crowd seem to be quite serious about it. There's opposition to it, of course, as you would expect, but from what I could find out, there's a good chance it will go ahead."

"Jesus! Can you imagine – a gold rush in Connemara? I wonder what that would do to the place?" Lyons said.

"Exactly. Of course, as usual, people seem to be divided. There are some that would do very well out of it – hotels, bars, restaurants, B&Bs and so on. But there's lots of folks who don't want the pristine beauty of the place disturbed, not to mention the nutters."

"Did you get the name of the mining company?"

"Yes. It's the Derivest Mining Corporation. They're based in Logan, Utah in the USA."

"OK. Well do a bit more exploration – excuse the pun – for me. I'll give Séan a call and tell him about it – see if he can find out anything out beyond."

"OK, boss. Thanks."

When Peadar Tobin had left the office, Lyons put a call through to Clifden.

She told Séan Mulholland what Tobin had found out and asked him whether he had heard anything about it.

"No, I can't say that I have, Maureen. But I'll have a dig around and see what I can find, if you pardon the pun."

Everyone's a wise guy, Lyons thought.

"OK, Séan, and let me know what you find out, if anything. Thanks."

* * *

The weather in Clifden had been holding up very well. September was often a fine month, giving the locals a chance to recharge their batteries before the south-westerly gales off the Atlantic set in for most of the winter. It was ironic that the good weather came as soon as the kids had gone back to school, but it seemed to happen that way every year.

Sergeant Mulholland told Jim Dolan that he was off out for a wander up the town, but didn't mention anything about his mission to discover if there was any truth in what Maureen Lyons had told him.

Mulholland was well known in Clifden, and well respected. He was a fair man, and while he wouldn't actually bend the law for anyone, he often interpreted it in a kindly fashion where no real malice was intended. But if anyone stepped seriously out of line, Mulholland would bring them to book in short order.

So it was that as he made his way past the various emporia that had quietened down significantly since the end of the main tourist season. He stopped to exchange a few pleasantries with the various traders and after a few minutes he came to the post office.

Bridget O'Toole was behind the counter and looked up when the little bell above the entrance tinkled.

"Ah, hello again, Séan. I've just put the kettle on for tea. Will you have a cup?"

"Hello, Bridget. Thanks, that would be very hospitable of you." He took a seat in the rather worn chair outside the counter that was placed there to facilitate the less able customers from the area.

Bridget disappeared into the back room, and returned a few moments later with two mugs of tea and a saucer of biscuits balanced delicately on top of one of them.

"It's great weather, Bridget. Have you been busy in the shop?" Mulholland asked, helping himself to two custard creams.

"Busy enough, now. But thankfully the sale of single stamps for postcards to America has slowed down a lot. Ye'd think they were buying the crown jewels the way some of them go on. And they'd keep ye nattering all the day long."

"I know what you mean. But they're good for the town. They bring a lot of trade, and sure aren't they nice and polite – well mostly anyway?"

"I suppose you're right. But it's been a long summer, Séan. I'm glad of a bit of peace and quiet to be honest."

"Tell me, Bridget, did you hear anything about some American outfit looking to do some mining or some such out near Ballyconneely?"

"God, I did. I thought it was a joke. Sure, there's nothing out there but old bog and rocks. But my daughter, Aoife, was up at the Alcock and Brown about a month ago and said there was an American guy waffling on about it. I think he'd had a bit too much Guinness, to be honest, but he had the locals in stitches."

"I see. I don't suppose Aoife got his name at all?"

"No, she didn't. She was with a few friends and they didn't pay him much mind, except that he was being a bit loud. What's your interest anyway, Séan?"

"Ah, 'tis probably nothing. The folks in Galway were asking about it, that's all. But it sounds like a tall tale from what you say. By the way, has there been any sign of young Davin Faherty since?" Mulholland said, deftly changing the subject.

"No, not a vestige. And, you know, his benefits will go out of date if he doesn't come and collect them soon, and then you can only guess at the amount of paperwork that will generate when he has to make a claim. Have you heard anything of him?"

"No, nothing. Ah, I suppose he's gone off to Dublin, or maybe further afield. You know what these young fellas are like. There's not much for the likes of him hereabouts anyway. Well, look, Bridget, I'd better get going. Thanks for the tea and the chat. Mind yourself now," he said getting up and placing his empty mug on the counter.

"Thanks, Séan. See you again soon."

Mulholland left the post office and continued up along the main street until he reached the Alcock and Brown Hotel. There was a pretty young blonde girl on reception with a badge stating that her name was Nikola. Mulholland assumed from the spelling that she hailed from Eastern Europe.

"Hello, Nikola. Have you got a minute?"

The girl was pleasant, but the sergeant could see from her eyes that she was nervous talking to the police.

"Yes, of course. How can I help?"

"Can I ask where you come from originally, Nikola?"

"I am Polish but my papers are all in order. I have them if you need to see them," the girl said with just a slight hint of an accent.

"No, no, that's not necessary," he said, smiling in an effort to reassure her. "Have you been here long?"

"I came at the start of the summer," she said.

"Ah, right. Have you enjoyed the work here?"

"Yes. I like meeting people, and the other staff are very nice. It's been busy, but it helps to make the day go quickly."

"Tell me, Nikola, have you had many American visitors in?"

"Oh, yes, lots. They usually stay just one or two nights, but they are very nice to deal with and sometimes leave good tips in the restaurant or the bar."

"Is there anyone that stands out in your mind for any reason?"

Nikola looked puzzled and thought for a moment before replying.

"Well, just Mr Gilbert. He has been here many times this year and he stays for a week or sometimes two. He's on his own when he comes. But he's very nice."

"And what strikes you as strange about Mr Gilbert?"

"It's just an unusual pattern, maybe it's not important."

"Could you look up Mr Gilbert's account and tell me how he pays, Nikola?"

The girl looked uneasy and said, "Maybe I should get the manager for you, officer."

"Ah, no, you're grand. I just want to know how he pays his bill. That's all. Nothing serious."

Nikola went to her computer and clicked a few keys.

"Yes, here it is. He pays by credit card. It's booked in the name of Deri... Derivest I think, and it's their card."

"Thanks, Nikola. Do you remember Mr Gilbert's first name?"

"Yes, he was Jed, Jed Gilbert."

"And is he staying here at the moment?"

"No. Let me see. He left about three weeks ago."

"Right. And is he booked in again for later in the year?"

Nikola tapped a few more keys on the keyboard of her computer.

"No, there is no future booking. Is that OK?"

"Yes, that's fine. Thanks very much, Nikola. Will you be staying on for the winter?"

"Yes, I hope so. Of course, it's not so busy, but there will be a few bookings until January. Is that OK?"

"Yes, that's not a problem, Nikola. Thanks for your help. I may see you again."

Chapter Six

"Mick, hi, it's me," Lyons said when she called the Detective Superintendent on his mobile. "Got a sec?"

"Sure, what's on your mind?"

Lyons went on to explain to her partner about the house out on the Newcastle Road.

"I was just wondering if you think we should get Liam and his gang in straight away, or should I get some of our own crew to mount an observation?" she said.

"Hmm... well, it's up to you, Maureen. You'll need to bring them in at some stage if there is something going on there, but I see your point. If you cry wolf too early and it turns out to be two old pensioners living there, you'll be a laughing stock for ages."

"That's why I wanted to ask for your input – and anyway, I just wanted to talk to you. We're both way too busy these days – we don't seem to have much time for each other."

"Yes, I know, and it's probably more my fault. I'm sorry, love. Look, let's see if we can arrange a few days off together. We could go to Paris or Madrid now that the fares have got cheap again. What do you say?"

"Yeah, sound great. Will I look into it?"

"No, leave it with me, I'll sort it. Are you OK with the other thing then?"

"Yes, thanks. I'll figure something out. See you later."

"Bye."

Despite what some might call Lyons' meteoric rise up through the ranks, she was often still a little unsure of her own abilities. She tried very hard not to let it show in front of her team, but she was glad that she had Mick Hays to call on for advice when she was feeling shaky about something. Her own self-doubt was quite unfounded. Ever since she had arrested a bank robber coming out of the TSB on Eyre Square as a rookie in uniform, she had gone on to run to earth many criminals, and had proven herself beyond any doubt to her superior officers. But still those nagging doubts remained.

She went in search of Eamon Flynn who was now in charge of the detectives since Lyons had assumed responsibility for the Serious and Organised Crime Unit in Galway.

When she found Flynn, she explained about their concerns that there was a cannabis factory out on the Newcastle Road, and asked if he could arrange some surveillance.

"Sally is getting in touch with the owner of a house opposite to see if we can use it. Have a word with her, will you?" Lyons said.

"Yes, OK. But don't you think we should get Liam involved, or at least let him know?" Flynn said.

Inspector Liam O'Higgins ran the drug detection unit attached to Mill Street Garda station in Galway. It was a busy posting, with the prevalence of drugs ever on the increase in the town. O'Higgins had a team of fifteen Gardaí at his disposal, but even so, he calculated that they were losing the battle with the dealers. Even when they made significant arrests, there always seemed to be a cohort of replacements available to the gangs to carry on the illegal trade. But despite this, O'Higgins had not become despondent, and he pursued his quarry with enthusiasm every single day.

"Let's just do some observation first. If it turns out to be nothing, we don't want to look stupid. Can you fix it up?"

"Yes, sure, no bother. I'll let you know when it's arranged."

"Thanks, Eamon."

* * *

Sally Fahy had managed to find the owner of the house on the corner of the Newcastle Road and had spoken to him. He was happy enough to allow the Gardaí to use the place as she suggested, and he wouldn't say anything to anyone. He was waiting for planning permission to come through so that he could redevelop the site, but it was a slow process. Sally arranged to collect a key from him at his office in Galway that afternoon, and he told her that there was a side entrance that opened onto the car park in front of the pharmacy, so they could get in without attracting attention.

As darkness fell upon the city, Sally Fahy and Eamon Flynn drove out to the junction where the alleged grow house was located and parked in front of the pharmacy.

"We'll need some provisions if we're going to be here for a while. Here's €20. Can you go and sort that while I find the back way into this place? I hope there aren't too many rats inside!" Flynn said mischievously, hoping to wind Sally up.

"Just one more won't make much of a difference then," she said, slapping Flynn affectionately on the hip.

"Cheeky!" Flynn said, getting out of the car.

Fahy went off to the Spar shop beside the pharmacy and bought a couple of pre-wrapped sandwiches, two chocolate bars and two bottles of soft drinks. She then made her way down the overgrown lane beside the empty house to the back door which Flynn had left ajar. Once inside, she secured it and went upstairs to the front room which looked out over the little cottage that they were proposing to watch.

The house was very musty, not having been aired for months, and the two Gardaí were reluctant to open a window in case anyone watching the grow house would notice and discover that the place was being observed.

There was still quite a bit of furniture in the old place, and a bookcase stacked with ageing paperbacks stood against the back wall of the room in which they had positioned themselves. But it was too dark to read the titles of the books, and they dared not use a torch in the gloom for obvious reasons.

Flynn carried in an old armchair for Sally to sit on, while he positioned himself on a stool that was covered in faded red velvet. Luckily, the front windows of the house were very dirty, and there were old, thin net curtains hanging down, so there was no chance that their presence could be detected from outside.

They had a good view of the entire area surrounding the small cottage. At first, a few people came and went to the take-away food shop beside their target property. At seven o'clock a small queue developed outside the premises, but it quickly cleared as the customers were supplied with their steaming hot fish, chips and burgers.

"It's well for some," Sally Fahy said to Flynn as the smell of the hot oil wafted across the street and in through their rather ill-fitting windows.

"Have your sandwich if you're hungry," Flynn said, "or if you like, you could sneak over there and get something hot for both of us."

"Better not. It would be just our luck if whoever is tending to that place turned up when I was gone. Have you got the camera primed and ready to go?"

"Yep. All fixed up."

They settled down in silence once again to await developments.

* * *

Maureen Lyons and Mick Hays had arrived home at nearly the same time not long after half past six. It was unusual, because more often than not one or other of them had to work on into the evening on some pressing matter. Lawlessness in Galway has no respect for the clock.

"I'm going to have a quick shower," Hays said, putting his briefcase down on the sofa in the sitting room.

"OK. I'll rustle us up some grub then. What do you fancy?"

"Have we any of that lasagne left in the freezer? It was very tasty."

"Yeah, I think so. Say, about twenty minutes?"

"Perfect!" Hays said, going over and giving her a quick kiss on the lips.

* * *

When they had eaten their fill of the pasta accompanied by a colourful salad and a nice bottle of pinot grigio, Hays sat back in the chair and said, "You know, Maureen, I've been thinking…"

"Oh-oh. Am I in trouble?"

"No, course not. No, I was having coffee with James McMahon the day before yesterday – you remember the architect bloke from before."

"Oh, yes, I do indeed remember Mr McMahon. What's he up to these days?"

"Ah, I think he's learnt his lesson with pretty young girls anyway. No, he was saying that this would be a great time to buy property in the city. He anticipates a serious capital appreciation coming over the next two to three years. Apparently, there are several new high-tech firms taking space around and about, and all their staff will be looking for rentals or houses to buy."

"I see. And we care because?"

"Well, this is what I was thinking. That place we have down by the river is doing great. It's returning eight percent gross just now – that's five percent net when the tax is paid. It's a lot more than you'd get in the bank."

"True. And it never seems to need anything much either. So, what were you thinking?"

"Well, we haven't touched the money we've received in rent over the last fifteen months. We could leverage that and get a mortgage to buy a second property, and rent it out. James would be able to point us in the right direction, I'm sure."

"I don't know, Mick. Are we really savvy enough to become property moguls? We've been lucky so far, but if it went wrong it could cost us dearly. And we're doing OK moneywise, in any case."

"Yeah, I know we are. But it would be a shame to miss an opportunity, and there doesn't seem to be much to it. Tell you what – why don't you give it some thought and we'll talk about it again in a few days?"

"OK. Sure. Anything good on telly this evening?" Lyons said, changing the subject.

"I was thinking we might have an early night," Hays said with a glint in his eye.

"Hmm... you know sometimes, Superintendent, you have some really bright ideas!"

Chapter Seven

Morgan Deri had come to America from Wales in the middle of the nineteenth century. At that time, there was almost no livelihood to be made in the Welsh hills other than by going down the mines, and Deri's health just wasn't up to that. To escape poverty and give himself and his wife Agnes some hope of a better future, they had set off by ship for what they thought of as the promised land.

Deri had ended up in Utah, in the foothills of the Oquirrh Mountains where the Green River carried small deposits of gold down to the valleys below. Deri had been quite unsuccessful at first, and both he and his wife almost starved, until he got the hang of panning for the fine deposits of ore and started to make good in a place he had been assured was barren.

Through tireless effort and unbridled optimism, Deri had persisted. The ground and the river running through it had begrudgingly given up its treasure, and after five years, Deri was in a position to buy some machinery and hire two other men. Things continued to improve for Deri, so that by the time the harsh Utah winters finally claimed him, he had built a small empire in mining and had fathered three strong sons with Agnes, who survived her husband by several years.

The sons had continued in their father's tradition and so it was that the Derivest Mining Corporation of Logan, Utah had grown into a multi-million-dollar enterprise with operations in the USA, Bolivia, Uganda and Scotland. Derivest specialized in long shots. They bought rights to mine in unlikely places where their chances of success were very limited, but when they did hit valuable minerals, the pay-off was substantial. As time went by, they got better at identifying likely sources of wealth, and employed the very best technology and the smartest geologists to improve their chances. It was a powerful strategy. None of the big mining companies were in the least bit interested in Derivest's claims, and they were able to function under the radar as it were, thus largely avoiding the quagmire of environmental pressure groups and conservationists that could slow an exploration down for years or even see it off altogether.

This was the approach that they were using in Connemara. Who could complain about some gentle probing of land that was unable to sustain any other kind of profitable activity, and the place was so underpopulated that there was hardly anyone to object in any case? But their scientists had told them that there were some valuable deposits in the ground there, and it was this that encouraged them to explore further.

* * *

Jed Gilbert parked his Ford in the lot at the back of the anonymous-looking concrete building just off Aggie Boulevard, near the University and close to the US-89 highway in Logan and got out. It was a fine autumn day, with just a hint of coolness in the gentle breeze, which was a welcome change after the searing heat of the summer months. As winter approached, the temperature would drop steeply from now on, and by Christmas, Logan would in all probability be covered in deep snow.

Jed made his way indoors, and was greeted by a number of colleagues as he went upstairs to the office of Chuck Deri, the CEO of Derivest, and great-grandson of Morgan Deri from Wales. Jed knocked on the door embellished with Chuck Deri's name in gold lettering in the shape of a rainbow on the top half of the door, which was ribbed glass.

"Come in, Jed, come in," boomed the voice of the CEO as he stood up slowly from his captain's chair behind the expansive desk that was littered with official-looking papers.

Chuck Deri was a large man in his mid-fifties. He was very much overweight, and his thinning grey hair arranged in a sort of comb-over did little to enhance the appearance of someone who clearly ate and drank rather too well for his health. His ruddy round face was clean-shaven, but his pale grey suit was having difficulty accommodating his significant bulk, and he had long since abandoned any attempt to wear a tie around his thick neck.

"Good to see you, Jed. Take a seat. Coffee?"

"Yes, thanks, Chuck. Just black, no sugar."

Chuck poured a mug of hot coffee from the contraption sitting on a stand nearby and handed it to Jed, before sitting down again and gesturing his visitor to do the same.

"So, how are things in the Emerald Isle?" Chuck said.

"Interesting, Chuck. I think we'll get there, but it's going to take a bit more time than we thought. Things move at a dreadfully slow pace in those parts. I did as you suggested. I dropped a good few dollars here and there among officialdom – brown envelopes they call it over there – and there doesn't seem to be too much opposition, or at least if there is, it's not well organised. Not yet anyway."

"Good. Sounds like progress. Do you think we'll be able to get started next summer on schedule?"

"I sure hope so. There is one slight snag though. There are two brothers running a small farmstead right where we want to start boring. I've spoken to them both. One of them is totally against us and the other is OK with it, and I've checked out their land rights, and it looks pretty watertight. I'm not sure yet how we're going to get around that one."

"Is the place valuable?" Chuck asked.

Jed sniggered.

"Not at all. It's a shit hole."

"Then just buy them out – it can't be worth much."

"It ain't that easy, Chuck. Some of these folks are mightily attached to their land. Something to do with Oliver Cromwell, whoever he is. They're not inclined to sell."

"God dammit, Jed, up the ante then. You know as well as I do that every man has his price. Just sort it out – whatever it takes. You know we need to get started there as soon as the weather clears next year, and I have a feeling it's going to be very worthwhile. Are you going back to Ireland again soon?"

"Yeah, I'll make another visit before the end of the year – see how things are going. There's some big meeting of the local politicians at the end of October, and they're going to decide about the license. I want to be there for that."

"Sounds good. Just make sure they come down on our side."

"Sure, Chuck. No problem."

* * *

It had been raining in Connemara solidly for three long days. It wasn't the misty drizzle that usually blew in from the Atlantic Ocean, but rather a solid heavy rain falling down vertically from the leaden sky overhead. The rain had swelled the hundreds of little streams that flowed down from the rocky hills into the myriad of lakes all over the territory around west Galway, north and east of Ballyconneely.

One such lake was Shannalecka Lough, which lay north of Boolagare and close to the Galway Mayo border. The land around the lake was accessed by an unmarked track, and like the bog, all over that area was now common land where local farmers could graze their hardy sheep all the year round.

Festus Greeley, now in his late sixties, with his mobility severely impaired due to arthritis brought on by the perpetually damp conditions in which he lived, had a small flock of sheep that grazed near the lake. In bad weather, Festus needed to keep an eye on the animals. You never knew when one would fall into a bog hole and be unable to climb out, and to lose even one of his beasts would be a costly affair for the man who lived on very meagre means.

With his trusty black and white collie dog, Shep, at his side, he donned his weatherproofs and cap and set off from the little cottage where he lived to check on the animals. It was still raining, but Festus was used to the weather, and although both Shep and himself were getting thoroughly soaked, they continued slowly out across the heathland counting the sheep marked with a distinctive dab of green paint on their fleeces. As they neared the lake itself, Festus noticed that one of the streams that emptied into it was providing only a trickle of mountain water, which should by rights have been a torrent. Fearing that one of his precious charges might be caught in the stream, he followed it up along for forty or fifty metres and came to a bend where a black plastic sack was stopping the water getting past. Shep went to investigate, and started barking wildly at the obstruction which caused Festus to look into it further. As he turned the bag over with the stout hawthorn stick that he always kept with him, it split open, and what appeared to be flesh stared up at the old farmer, causing him to step back hastily, losing his footing and landing on his rear end in the marshy ground.

Shep was still barking at the apparition, never having seen a dead human before, and Festus prised himself up of the wet ground till he was standing again, and summoned the dog who came willingly to his side.

"Good God, Shep, this is a right how do you do. We'd better get back and get some help. The poor fella. We can't leave him here."

Festus had no telephone in his rather squalid little cottage, and mobile phones were a total mystery to the man who simply didn't understand how a thing without wires could send messages and let you speak to anyone. It was beyond his understanding. But his neighbour did have a telephone, so Festus made his way slowly to the nearby homestead that was in better shape than his own, and told the man what he had found. Together, they called Clifden Garda station, but not before Festus had been reinforced with a large tot of poitín to help him over the shock.

Chapter Eight

Maureen Lyons was sitting in her office daydreaming. The persistent rain had dampened her spirits somewhat, but she was thinking about what Mick Hays had said the previous evening regarding investing in property, and she was confused. His proposition looked sound enough from what he had said, but she was cautious. She came from the school that thought if it sounds too good to be true, then it probably is. But Mick was a good judge, and not at all impetuous, so she figured if he felt OK about it, then she should perhaps go along with the idea. They would have no trouble getting a loan, and McMahon, whatever else he was, had a good handle on the property scene in the western capital, and could almost certainly steer them in the right direction.

Lyons' thoughts were punctuated by the telephone.

"Lyons," she said, quickly focusing back on her job.

"Maureen, it's Seán. Listen, I've had a call from Festus Greeley. He keeps a few sheep out near Shannalecka. He was tending to them this morning when he came across what he thinks might be a body wrapped in plastic in one of the little rivers flowing down into the lake."

"Crikey. Do you think this Festus what's-his-name is reliable, Seán?"

"Ah, I'd say so. I don't know him well, but I'd say he's sound enough."

"OK. So, have you been out there yourself?"

"Ah, no, Maureen. It's very rough terrain out that way, and what with my bad knee it wouldn't be any good me going out there. But I could send Jim Dolan out – what do you think?"

Lyons turned around so that she could study the Ordnance Survey map that was pinned up on the wall of her office.

"Is that place not in County Mayo, Seán?"

"No, it's still Galway just there. It's near the county boundary all right, but I'm afraid it's on our patch still."

"Right. Well best get Jim out there then. I'll come out too with Sally. We'll leave the forensics till we have established what's what. And get Jim to send me the grid reference or I'll be driving around all bloody day trying to find the place."

"Better bring your Wellington boots too, Maureen. 'tis fierce damp out today."

"Terrific. Thanks, Seán. Talk soon."

* * *

Lyons collected Sally Fahy from the open plan office and they set off out west in Lyons' car. The weather was truly awful, and driving conditions were very poor, so Lyons took it easy till they were past Moycullen when she could speed things up a bit. But the constant heavy rain still made things difficult, and the wipers, even set to their highest speed, had trouble keeping the windscreen clear enough for safe navigation.

"How did you and Eamon get on last night, Sally?"

"OK, thanks. There's definitely something very dodgy going on at that place beside the chemists on the Newcastle Road."

"What did you see?"

"We stayed till just after twelve. At around eleven-fifteen a guy in a grey hoodie came shuffling along looking all around him and behaving very furtively. He walked up past the cottage and then did a one-eighty and came back and let himself in. He stayed inside for twenty minutes or so and then came back out and disappeared very quickly."

"Did you get a look at his face?" Lyons said.

"No chance. He kept it well hidden. But I'd say he was in his late twenties or early thirties, and fit, judging by the speed he was walking at."

"OK, well when we get back, you'd better give Liam a call and put him in the picture. But don't let him steal the whole gig. We found the place after all, and I want some of the credit."

"OK, boss. I hear what you're saying."

"And how did you get on with Eamon?"

"How do you mean?" Fahy said.

"Well, just the two of you, stuck in that place in the dark. Nothing much happening. You know."

"Give over, will you. If I wanted to snag Eamon Flynn, it wouldn't be on a stake-out in a filthy old property with the smell of fried food wafting in on the breeze."

"Oh yeah! And do you?"

"Do I what?" Fahy said.

"Do you want to snag Eamon?"

"Only if I get desperate," the pretty blonde detective answered, and they both laughed.

* * *

By the time the two detectives had arrived at the turn off for Shannalecka, the weather had changed. The persistent downpour had given way to a fine mist being blown horizontally across the bog by a strong westerly wind.

Lyons and Fahy drove up along the old track towards the location that had been sent to her phone, and soon enough, Jim Dolan's pale blue Ford Mondeo came into view. As Lyons pulled up beside it, hoping that her Volvo wouldn't sink into the soft ground, they got out.

Lyons and Fahy covered themselves against the weather as best they could. Dolan already had his wet gear on, so he waited patiently on the leeward side of his car until they were all ready.

"It's over here," Dolan shouted, his words being carried away on the stiff breeze, but his arm was waving in the right direction.

The three made their way slowly forward, trying to avoid slipping into the treacherous bog pools. They came to rest at a bend in the stream that was feeding the lake, and looked down to see a large black object stuck in the flow. Water had built up behind the black plastic object, and it was torn here and there, giving a glimpse of sodden clothing and what could have been human skin.

"Crikey, Jim. Can you get down into the stream and see if you can lift that up, whatever it is?"

"Right, boss."

Dolan, who thankfully had equipped himself with Wellington boots, stood down into the flowing stream, and tried to get to grips with the shiny, slippery object. He wrestled with it this way and that, but after a few minutes he had done nothing but rotate the black plastic over on itself in the water.

"It's no use," he shouted from his position bent over it, "I can't get a decent grip on it. We'll have to get help."

"Shit. And where do you suggest we do that, Jim?" Lyons said, struggling to be heard.

"It's OK, boss. I'll go and get someone with a tractor or something. You stay here," Fahy said.

"Oh, right, Sally. You just go off in my nice warm, dry car, and I'll stay out here in the pissing rain with Jim and catch pneumonia!"

"No, boss, you can sit in Jim's car. I won't be long."

Fahy got into Lyons' car and started it. She had to rock the Volvo to and fro a few times to free it from the mud, but after a few goes she had it turned around and was heading back down along the rutted track. Lyons and Dolan sat into his car and started the engine, setting the heater on maximum to start the drying out process.

"Did you get a look at what's in the sack, Jim?"

"No, not properly. But chances are it's a body all right. We won't know for sure until we get it out. Do you want to get forensics to attend?"

"Yeah, I suppose so. I just hope to God it's not a sheep! Will you call Séan and ask him to get a uniformed officer out in a car to close off the entrance to the lane? The last thing we need is rubberneckers."

"Yeah, OK, though I think we're safe enough in this weather. Still, best to be sure."

* * *

Fahy drove back onto the proper road and turned left. She was conscious of the closeness of the Mayo border, and she didn't want to complicate matters by seeking help from an adjoining Garda district, though she wasn't sure that it would actually matter in the end. She drove for about 500 metres and came to a cottage set back from the road with a large steel shed beside it where she could see a weather-beaten old red tractor peeking out.

She spoke to the old man who was inside the little house in front of a nice warm turf fire having a cup of tea, and asked if his machine would be able to help them raise a large bag out of the stream.

The old man assured her that his old tractor was just the thing for the job. He spent a good ten minutes damping down the fire and equipping himself for the hostile weather, and then, accompanied by his own black and white sheepdog, walked over to the barn and started the Massey Ferguson tractor which turned over six times before catching and emitting a large cloud of blue smoke.

Fahy set off slowly back to the site, followed by the red tractor bouncing around on the uneven ground.

When they turned down along the narrow track leading to Shannalecka, the lane was still unguarded, and after a few minutes they arrived back where Dolan's car was parked with all the windows steamed up.

The farmer took a few minutes to position his machine with its rear end facing the bend in the river. He attached broad canvas straps to the hydraulic arms protruding from the rear of the old machine and slid down into the torrent. After a few minutes he had struggled with the bag and managed to wrap the straps around it. Jim Dolan helped him to scramble back up. He went to the front of the machine and advanced the throttle on the old thing, operating a lever on the footplate to slowly bring up the hoist.

The farmer, who was quite used to retrieving animals from bog holes, was adept at manoeuvring his equipment, and soon had the bag sitting on the bank and was removing the straps.

Fahy took the man's details, and let him away. He didn't ask any questions, and the Gardaí felt that he was quite happy to be getting back to the warmth of his little house.

When he had gone, Dolan pulled back a little of the plastic wrapping and revealed the head of a young man, bloated and blue from being in the water.

Chapter Nine

Jim Dolan had put the call in to the Garda forensic unit, and Sinéad Loughran had said that she would leave right away to come out to the site. When Lyons got back into her car, she called the pathologist, Dr Julian Dodd, and put him in the picture.

"And you expect me to come out to the back of beyond in this weather, I suppose, Inspector?" Dodd said, not relishing either the journey, nor the investigation that would inevitably follow if what they had found was in fact a corpse.

"Well, we need someone to certify that he's dead, doctor, and there may well be evidence as to how he came to be deceased, so, yes, I'm afraid your presence is required," Lyons said, in no frame of mind to humour the doctor on this occasion.

"Very well. I'll be out presently then," he said with a sigh, "try not to mess the scene up too much till I get there."

"Of course not. See you soon," Lyons said.

Dr Julian Dodd was a man of diminutive stature who was always immaculately turned out and had a dry, rather ironic turn of phrase. But he was an excellent pathologist, and for that reason the detectives tolerated his somewhat odd manner as he went about his gruesome profession. He had often been able to find little pieces of evidence that helped to convict wrongdoers where others might have missed them altogether, or dismissed them as being of little consequence. To say that he enjoyed his work might be going a bit far, but he was very professional and invariably reliable.

The three detectives sat into Lyons' car to await the arrival of the SOCO unit, which they estimated would take a good forty minutes, if not a bit longer given the poor driving conditions.

"What do you reckon, Sally; Jim?" Lyons said, turning sideways so that she could see her colleagues.

"Have we any missing person reports from the area?" Jim Dolan said.

"Good point, Jim. Can you give Séan a call and ask him to have a look for us. What do you think, Sally?"

"Wasn't there some talk of one of the Faherty brothers going walkabout? I wonder, could that be him?"

"Yes, I thought of that too. But it's a bit of a leap. Better wait till Sinéad gets here and see if there's any identification on him before jumping to conclusions. I presume there's no doubt that it is a man, Jim?" Lyons said.

"There's two or three days of stubble on its face – so I'd say that's not in doubt."

* * *

The weather was still dreadful as Sinéad Loughran's 4x4 came swaying across the rough terrain and pulled up alongside Lyons' car. Loughran got out and came across, getting into the back of the Volvo alongside Jim Dolan.

"Hi, folks. Grand day for it – not! What have you got for me?"

"It's over there beside the stream, wrapped in a black plastic sack. Looks like the body of a man. Dodd is on his way too. Do you want to wait till he gets here?" Lyons said.

"No. May as well make a start. Not much chance of being able to erect a tent in this wind. Best just brave the elements and see what we can find."

Sinéad Loughran got out of the car again, and signalled to her two colleagues in the jeep to join her at the side of the stream where the body lay. Handling the corpse gently, and with some dignity, they turned the man over and straightened out his limbs so that he was lying on his back. Loughran placed his hands in a folded position on his chest, so that he looked like he was in repose. She closed his eyelids down, before gently starting to cut the plastic from around the body and lay it aside.

The body was fully clothed in blue jeans, a green pullover on top of a plain twill shirt, and was wearing what looked like expensive, but badly stained trainers.

Loughran fished in his jeans pockets and retrieved a wallet. She walked over to where Lyons was observing through the open window of her car, and handed it to her.

"There may be something useful in this," Loughran said, handing the wallet to Lyons who was hastily donning vinyl gloves.

Inside, there was a small green Public Services Card showing a picture of the deceased in better times, and identifying him as none other than Davin Faherty.

"Any idea how long he's been there, Sinéad?"

"Well, rigor mortis is gone, so he's been dead for more than thirty-six hours at least, but could be a good bit longer. Better wait for the doctor for anything more precise. And he may not have died here either. We won't know that till we get him back to Galway and do a thorough examination."

"OK. What are you going to do now?"

"We're going to do a search of the riverbank in case there's any evidence to retrieve. I'll take a wander back up along too. He may have been killed further up the hill and there could be some signs of whatever happened. Want to come?" Loughran said.

"Christ, Sinéad, you bring me to the nicest places!"

"Aw, come on, the rain is good for your skin!" Loughran said with a wide grin opening the door of Lyons' Volvo.

As they trudged up by the stream which was now flowing freely back on its original course, the obstruction having been removed, Lyons said to her colleague, "Any sign of an injury to the body?"

"Nothing obvious. But you need to wait for Dodd to have a look. I don't want to be accused of stealing his thunder. Speaking of which–"

The two women turned around to see Dr Julian Dodd's car wallowing across the bog towards the place where the body was lying. They kept going on up the incline towards the peak of the little hill. As they got to the top, Loughran bent down on her hunkers and started looking closely at the rough ground.

"Could be something here, Maureen," she said, pointing to where the moss and reeds seemed to be all scuffed up, exposing the dark brown peat beneath.

"OK. I won't come any closer just in case. Do you want me to send up one of the others?"

"Yes, thanks. And ask him to bring a few evidence bags and his camera. I think something happened around here."

* * *

"Good afternoon, Inspector. I do wish you'd stop finding bodies in these inaccessible places. And as for the weather – don't get me started!" Dr Julian Dodd said, although he wasn't as grumpy as he could have been under the circumstances.

"Hello, doctor. Just give me a minute to organise a few things, and then I'll be with you."

Lyons went and spoke to one of the other forensic team and relayed Loughran's request to him. He collected the items from the jeep and set off, clad in a white scene-of-crime suit, up towards Loughran who was waiting at the crest of the hill.

Lyons walked back to where the doctor was bent down over his charge, kneeling on the plastic sheet, examining the body.

"I don't know, and I don't know," he said as Lyons approached.

Lyons looked at the man, puzzled.

"Well, you are about to ask me how he died and when, so I thought I'd get my answers in first," Dodd said with a slight smirk.

"I see. Well, what can you tell me then?" she said, her patience wearing a little thin as a stream of rainwater ran down the back of her neck under her collar.

"He's definitely deceased – that's about it, till I get him back and get busy. Shall we say ten o'clock tomorrow?" the doctor said getting up and putting his stuff away.

"Is that it?" Lyons said incredulously.

"Yes, Inspector. That's it. I have fulfilled my statutory obligation by declaring the man dead, and now I want to get away from this godforsaken place as quickly as I can."

"Is there any sign of injury on the body, doctor?"

"None clearly visible, not about his head in any case, Inspector, but as I said, tomorrow morning – we'll all learn much more then, I imagine."

The doctor picked his way as carefully as he could back to his black Lexus, which was now splattered with mud, and got in. Although he had some difficulty getting the car pointing towards civilization, with the wheels spinning on the soft ground covering more of the car in dirt, he finally got matters under control, and set off at a gentle pace back across the bog.

Lyons watched him go, feeling quite frustrated at the lack of information he had provided.

She then sat back into her car and spoke to Jim Dolan and Sally Fahy.

"Sally, can you and Jim drive over to the Faherty farm. We had better inform Davin's brother of what we have found – but don't be too specific. I want you both to watch his reaction carefully. See what he has to say, and find out when he actually saw Davin for the last time, and what the circumstances were."

"As in, did they have a fight? That sort of thing," Dolan said.

"Yes, exactly. He'll hardly come straight out with it, so use your loaf and read between the lines. Have a good look around too. I think Davin was driving a black Golf. See if there's any sign."

"OK, boss. What are you going to do?" Fahy asked.

"I'm going into Clifden. I want to talk to Séan about all this. He has local knowledge. Let's see if we can find out what's really going on. Give me a call when you're done with Faherty and we'll arrange to meet up for the drive back to town."

"Right. See you later," Fahy said, and they got out of Lyons' car and went across to Dolan's blue Mondeo.

Chapter Ten

When Jim Dolan and Sally Fahy arrived at the Faherty farm, Dolan drove into the yard and stopped close to the house. The rain had started again, but it wasn't particularly heavy – just wet.

Dolan thumped on the door of the house with his fist a few times, and stood in close to the building to try and avoid getting soaked. There was no sound from within, so after a minute or two, he used his knuckles to rap more urgently on the wooden door.

"Mr Faherty. Laughlin, are you there? It's the police," Dolan said in a loud voice. But there was still no response.

Fahy had got out of the car and had made her way over to the large barn at the other side of the farmyard. An old muddy Land Rover was standing in front of the barn, so she took the torch from her waistband and went inside. The barn was cavernous in size – rather too large for the enterprise, she thought. Towards the front there was a middle-aged Massey Ferguson tractor parked, and Fahy put her hand on the engine which was cold to the touch. She went further in, going behind the machine. Towards the back of the shed, she could make out a shape with a dirty grey canvas tarpaulin draped over it. She approached, and lifted the corner of the cover up. Underneath, she could see that there was quite a smart-looking black VW Golf. She made a note of the registration and took a photograph of it with her phone. Then she went in search of her colleague.

"Jim. Jim, over here," she called.

Dolan came over to the entrance to the barn to join her.

"Look what I found inside," she said, holding out her phone with the picture of the front of the Golf.

"Cripes. Isn't that the type of car Davin was driving?"

"Yes, I think so. I'll give John O'Connor a call and ask him to check out the number. Did you find the brother?" Fahy said.

"No, he's not in."

"Does he have a car too, or is that old jeep it?"

"Dunno. Chances are he's out in the fields somewhere. Maybe we should go and see if we can find him," Dolan said.

"Hang on a sec. John's on the line."

Fahy gave O'Connor the registration number of the car she had found, and he asked her to hold on. A moment later he was back.

"Sarge, that car is registered to a girl who lives here in Galway. I had a quick look on Facebook. She's a nurse, and from her latest posts it looks like she's gone to Australia."

"Thanks, John. I think someone said that Davin had bought the car from Tadgh Deasy, and that it used to belong to a nurse. Can you let the inspector know that we've found it out at the Faherty farm under a cover in the barn? Tell her there's no sign of the brother either, and we're going out across the fields to see if we can find him."

"OK, Sarge, mind how you go."

Fahy and Dolan put on their wet gear, locked up Dolan's car and set off along the narrow path that led to the few fields attached to the farm.

* * *

They found Laughlin Faherty mending a dry-stone wall where one of the sheep had knocked part of it down in its quest for some better grazing. He saw the two Gardaí approaching, and stood up, putting his hand on the small of his back where it was a little stiff from bending over for so long.

"Good morning, Laughlin. That's a fine job you're doing there. Quite a skill fixing up those dry walls. Can we have a word?" Fahy said.

"Yeah, I could do with a break actually. What's on your mind?"

"I'm sorry to tell you, Laughlin, but a body was found up by Shannalecka lake and we have reason to believe it may be your brother, Davin."

Fahy and Dolan waited for the news to sink in before she went on, "Of course, we'll need confirmation, but we found his Public Services Card in his wallet, and there seems to be little doubt."

Laughlin Faherty showed no emotion as he digested the information. He just stood there staring at the ground, and said nothing.

"I wonder if we could go back to the house, Laughlin? We need to ask you a few questions."

Faherty still said nothing. He collected up the few tools he had brought with him to re-instate the wall, and set off down along the ditch towards the farm. Fahy looked at Dolan and shrugged, and followed on behind.

* * *

Ten minutes later Fahy and Dolan were seated close to the hearth in the Faherty farm. Laughlin had tickled the fire into life with the poker, and had put some dry turf on it which was beginning to catch, giving out a sweet smell and quite a bit of heat.

"Can I get you some tea?" Laughlin said.

"Yes, thanks, Laughlin, that would be lovely," Jim Dolan said.

"I'm sorry, I have no biscuits or anything. I have to go into the shops later and get some stuff."

"Ah, don't worry, Laughlin, just the tea will be grand. Is that your old Land Rover out in the yard?"

Faherty looked at Jim Dolan as if he was some kind of idiot.

"Sure, who else do you think owns it?"

Dolan didn't reply, but waited till Laughlin had filled the teapot and brought it to the table along with a bottle half full of milk and a bag of sugar. He poured out the tea for all three of them.

"Laughlin, when did you last see your brother?" Fahy said.

"It must be more than a week since. He comes and goes as he pleases. I don't monitor his movements."

"So, can you say when exactly it was when you last saw him?"

"No. Like I said, a week at least, maybe more."

"Was he here?"

"Yes, of course. Where else would I see him?"

"Were you on good terms?" Fahy said.

"Look, Guard, I'm sure you know, Davin and me never got on. Not since we were small. We have very different ideas about just about everything. So he went his way, and I went mine. Don't get me wrong. If he's dead, I'm sorry – he was my brother after all, but to answer your question, no, we weren't on good terms."

"What kind of car did Davin drive, Laughlin?" Fahy said.

"I dunno. Some black thing. It might be a Volkswagen. I'm not good with cars."

"Laughlin, there's a black Volkswagen Golf out in your barn with a canvas tarpaulin over it. Is that Davin's car?"

"It's not just my barn. He lived here too, you know."

"Yes, but how come it's in there, and under a cover too?" Dolan said.

"How should I know? He must have left it there for some reason," Laughlin said rather sourly.

"Yes, but it's a bit strange, don't you think? I mean how come his car is tucked up in the barn and he's lying in a stream out in the bog several miles away?"

"Look, officer, I've told you, me and him weren't close. I have no idea what he was up to or how he got to wherever. Now, if that's all, I need to get on. There's work to be done."

"Mr Faherty, I'm afraid we'll have to ask you to leave your vehicle here while our forensic team have a look over it. Just routine, you understand. We should be able to release it back to you later on," Fahy said.

"Suit yourselves."

"And we'll need you to come into Galway tomorrow to formally identify your brother. We'll send a car for you," Dolan said.

"Make it good and early. I have a lot of work to do getting things ready for the winter out here."

"Right. We'll leave you in peace then," Dolan said, and they got up from the table and went outside.

Once they were clear of the house, Sally Fahy said, "I'll just give Sinéad Loughran a call and ask her to send someone down to go over the Land Rover. What do you reckon?"

"God, I don't know, Sally. It all seems a bit dodgy to me. I mean the lad's car is here all covered up like that. I'd say he knows more than he's letting on, but without any hard evidence, we'll have to leave him alone for now. Let's see what forensics can pull up from the Land Rover."

As they sat back into Dolan's car, Laughlin Faherty came out of the house and walked back up the path leading to his fields.

Chapter Eleven

Inspector Liam O'Higgins climbed the stairs two at a time at Mill Street Garda station. He knocked on Lyons' door.

"Hi, Liam, come in. Good to see you. Take a pew," she said gesturing towards the chair in front of her desk.

"Hi, Maureen, thanks. How are things?"

"Ah, you know, busy busy. Can I get you a coffee or tea?"

"No, you're grand. So what's the craic?"

"Very drole, Liam, very drole." She went on to fill the drugs detective in on what had been observed out on the Newcastle Road.

"Now, don't get me wrong, we don't want to eat your lunch, but I'd like to maintain an interest in the place and whatever you find there," Lyons said.

"OK. Why the concern?"

"I can't put my finger on it – call it woman's intuition, if you like. I just have a feeling that it's somehow important. What do you say?"

"Hmm... OK. I don't mind you tagging along. It will take us a while to get to the point where we want to go in and make arrests. We need to try and find out who the Mr

Big in this is. The guy that comes to tend to the plants is hardly a mastermind."

"Thanks. I'll ask Sally Fahy to liaise with your folks. She was the one who did the obbo on the place and she's a very good officer."

"Fine. I hope she doesn't mind late nights!"

Lyons looked at O'Higgins and smiled.

"No, she'll be fine with that. Let me brief her later on and then I'll get her to call you. Is there much of this kind of thing going on in Galway?"

"Seems that it's increasing. The demand for weed is growing – forgive the pun – but in a university town, it's what you can expect. There's a lot more money to be made if you actually grow the stuff, and you can regulate the quality more easily too. So, yes, we have uncovered one or two of them over the past couple of years. To be honest I wish they would legalize the stuff. Then we could get on and deal with the really harmful drugs like cocaine and heroin."

"Do you think they will? Legalize it, I mean."

"Definitely. It's only a matter of time. But it's not a high priority for the politicians at the moment. But we are lobbying them every chance we get. It's crazy having uniformed Gardaí arresting some nineteen-year-old with a score bag in his jeans and bringing him before the courts where the officer has to spend a whole day only for the young fella to get a ten euro fine. Ridiculous! But when it's happening on an industrial scale, that's different. We need to deal with that because it leads to all sorts of aggravation."

"Any idea who might be behind this lot?" Lyons said.

"Not yet. But we'll get them, don't worry. They eventually start to think they are invincible and make mistakes – just like the criminals you chase down. I heard about your triumph with the ATMs – nice one!"

"Ah, it was a team effort, Liam. But glad we got them anyway. They were giving an entirely new meaning to 'hole in the wall'!"

The two inspectors laughed at that.

"Well, I'd better get going, Maureen. Good to catch up. I'll wait to hear from Sarah later on," O'Higgins said, getting up to leave.

"It's Sally – Sally Fahy, Liam."

"Oh, right, Sally. Like Aunt Sally. I'll remember."

"She's no one's aunt, Liam. In fact, I'd say your guys had better watch themselves. If they get on the wrong side, surgery will be required!"

"Nice. OK, I'll tell them. See you soon."

* * *

Lyons was just settling back at her desk when her phone rang.

"Lyons."

"Hi, Maureen. It's Sinéad. Look, I have the report from the examination of Laughlin Faherty's Land Rover. Is it OK if I pop over?"

"Yeah sure – oh, and bring some coffee and a doughnut, will you?"

"Sure. That bad is it?"

"Ah, ye know."

A few minutes later, Sinéad Loughran arrived at Lyons' office laden down with two paper cups of coffee in a cardboard tray, a white paper bag of cakes and with a folder tucked under her arm.

"Great! Thanks, you're a life saver."

"No problem."

The two women set about the coffee and doughnuts, with Lyons having to frequently wipe sugar and cream from her mouth with a tissue as she tucked into the delicious snack. When she had finished eating, she said, "Where did you manage to grab these? They're fabulous!"

"There's a new little bakery just around the corner and they're out to impress."

"Oh, I hadn't spotted that. Well done you."

"Some detective you are, Maureen Lyons," Sinéad said, smirking. "Anyway, do you want to see what's in the report?"

"Not really, but I suppose I must. Go on then."

"I'm afraid it's inconclusive. Davin's fingerprints are in the vehicle, but mostly on the bare metal close to the front passenger's seat. There were one or two on the rear door as well, but they are perfectly clear, indicating that it's just from normal handling. Not like he was resisting being pushed in or anything."

"Go on."

"The load area was a bit better. We found a few hairs that matched Davin's down the back of the floor covering, and there was some blood too – but it turned out to be of the animal kind. Oryctolagus cuniculus to be exact – that's rabbit to you and me."

"Great! What did the poor devil die of anyway?"

"Did you not get Dodd's report?" Loughran said.

"No, I didn't see it come in."

"Oh, right. Admin cock-up then. I'll make sure you get a copy as soon as I go back. But anyway, Davin Faherty, it appears, died from arsenic poisoning. It's a bugger to detect, so we had to send blood samples and tissue from his inside bits away for analysis, but that's what came back."

"Shit. Right. I wonder how he got that then?"

"That's the problem. Arsenic is pretty well all around us, but thankfully not in lethal doses. It could be in the water out there if they have a well, and of course it's commonly found anywhere there is mining – especially for copper or precious metals."

"Thanks a bunch, Sinéad. You know there is a mining connection to that place, I suppose?"

"No, I didn't. How come?"

Lyons went on to explain about Derivest and their interest in exploring the ground all over the area.

"Cripes. Well, if they have been taking core samples, and were careless about discarding them, some arsenic could easily have got into the water. What do you want to do?"

"Yeah, but if he died of arsenic poisoning from the water, who wrapped him up in black plastic and dumped him in the river? Let's go back out to Boolagare and see where the Fahertys' water supply comes from. If you bring your magic kit can you analyse the water for arsenic on the spot?"

"Yes, I can get a special sampler from the lab. Give me half an hour and then we can go if you like?"

"Yes, fine. Call me from downstairs when you're ready."

* * *

Lyons spent the half hour briefing Sally Fahy on her discussion with Liam O'Higgins. Fahy was pleased to be included in the action, and said that she was looking forward to working with the drugs team to see if they could apprehend those responsible for the weed factory.

"Just be a bit careful with these guys, Sally."

"How do you mean?" Fahy asked.

"Well, firstly they have a bit of a rep for the ladies, you know."

"It's OK, Inspector, I have a gun!"

"Hmm... right, that should take care of that problem then. But they'll also try to grab all the credit if you are successful."

"Refer to previous comment, boss."

Lyons laughed. "OK, but just remember that when you shoot a fellow officer, the paperwork is horrendous."

The two women laughed.

Chapter Twelve

Jed Gilbert took the company limousine from his home to Logan-Cache Airport. When he was dropped off, he went into the main building and walked over to the Utah Air Taxi desk and introduced himself. He knew the girl on reception pretty well by now – Derivest used this service regularly to transport their personnel to Salt Lake City International Airport, some seventy miles away.

"Good afternoon, Mr Gilbert. Heading to Salt Lake today?" said a girl who had a badge announcing her name as Scarlett pinned to her jacket.

"Hi, Scarlett. Yes, that's it. Is he ready?"

"I'll just check for you," Scarlett said, lifting the phone and calling the operations room.

"Hi, Josh, this is Scarlett. I have Mr Gilbert here from Derivest. He's ready to go if you are?"

"OK. Send him out to the plane. I'll meet him there."

Scarlett hung up and directed Jed Gilbert to the plane which was standing outside on the apron in the early morning sunshine.

"Which one is it today, Scarlett?"

"Oh, it's the blue one. Josh will be with you in a minute. He'll load your bag. You have a nice flight now."

"Thanks."

Gilbert walked out to the Cessna 340 twin-engined machine and met up with Josh. A couple of minutes later the two men were onboard, the engines had been started, and they were on their way. The flight to Salt Lake City International Airport would only take thirty-five minutes, and they would land on the general aviation runway and taxi to the main terminal where Jed would transfer to the United service to Newark, with a flight time of just over four hours.

From Newark, after a five-hour stop-over, Jed would board the United 767 for Shannon Airport on the west coast of Ireland. That flight would be through the night, arriving in Shannon in the early hours of the following day. Jed had reserved seat 4A in Polaris Business Class, which provided a lie-flat bed for the journey once the evening meal had been served and cleared away.

* * *

Lyons and Loughran drove out along the old bog road to Boolagare. They pulled Lyons' Volvo into the yard of the Faherty farm and got out. The weather was holding up reasonably well. It was overcast, but the clouds were high, and it looked as if it would stay fine for the rest of the day, although you could never be sure in this part of the country.

Lyons went to the front door of the house and rapped on the wooden door. There was no response, and she could hear no sounds.

"Looks like he's not here, Sinéad. There's no sign of the Land Rover either. He must be away somewhere."

"Never mind. I'll have a look around and see if I can spot where the water is going into the house, and trace it back. I doubt if they are on a mains supply here."

"OK. I'll come with you."

The women went to the back of the house and found a black poly pipe coming up from the ground and going inside through a hole in the wall that had been roughly plastered up to keep out mice or other rodents.

"It must be around here somewhere, Maureen. Have a look down there and see if you can see anything."

Lyons walked away from the house down a gentle incline and came to a point where she could see a round concrete cover about the size of a dustbin lid, almost buried in greenery – mostly weeds. A black plastic pipe was protruding from the vessel and went underground almost immediately pointing towards the dwelling.

"Over here. I think I've found it," Lyons shouted to Sinéad, who was looking in the opposite direction. She came and joined Lyons beside the well.

"Let's see if we can get the cover off. Then I can try and get a sample," Loughran said.

Lyons donned vinyl gloves to protect her hands and the two women bent down and struggled to prise the lid off the opening, to no avail.

"It's no use. I'll have to get a jemmy or something. Hang on, I'll have a look in the barn," Loughran said, straightening up. She walked off and into the darkness of the large shed where a variety of equipment including a good array of tools was located. She rooted around in the shed using her phone as a torch, and saw a large steel toolbox on the ground underneath a rough wooden bench. Loughran bent down and opened the box and took out a wrecking bar that was half a meter long and had a hook at one end.

Back outside, she waved the iron bar at Lyons.

"This should do it."

"Great. Let's have another go."

After a few minutes, the women had lifted the cover off the well, and were shining both of their torches into the abyss.

"Looks like there's a submerged pump in the bottom. Have you got something to dip in to get a sample of water?" Lyons asked.

"I'll have to improvise. Give me a minute."

Loughran went back to the car and spent a few minutes fiddling around, returning to where Lyons was standing with a small glass bottle with a bright orange string attached to the neck.

"I'll drop this in and hopefully it will fill with water."

Loughran dropped the bottle into the darkness and heard the plop as it hit the water. She left it in place for a moment or two, allowing the bottle to turn over and fill, or partly fill, with the well water. Then she gently hauled it up and stood holding out the nearly full receptacle triumphantly.

"There ya go! Fancy a drink?"

"No thanks. Not until you've checked it for arsenic anyway," Lyons said smiling.

"Give me a few minutes," Loughran said, walking back towards Lyons' car carrying the sample of well water.

Lyons walked back to where Loughran was working out of the boot of the car.

"What have you there, Sinéad?"

"It's a rapid testing kit for arsenic. You drop a sachet of this stuff into the water and wait till it goes a kind of yellow colour, then this chart tells me how much arsenic there is in the water," she said, holding up a card with progressively darker squares of yellow ink along the base.

"How much is safe?"

"They reckon point one milligrams per litre is OK – but that's very conservative. I would be happy with point two, but anything more than that and I'd want to filter it before I drank it."

"Does a water filter remove it?" Lyons said.

"Yes. A decent reverse osmosis filter will neutralise it as long as you remember to change the filter regularly. Hang on, I think it's finished."

Loughran held up the water in the bottle against the light which had now gone a pale yellow colour. She compared the colour of the water to the chart.

"Hmm. Just on the edge, I'd say. I wonder if they have a filter indoors."

"Is it enough to poison someone?"

"No, not at all. Not even after prolonged ingestion. But it wouldn't do you any good. I wonder if it has always been like that, or just since that mining company started taking core samples. That could cause some of this stuff to leach into the water."

"I think we need to talk to the mining company, don't you?" Lyons said.

"That's your department, Maureen. I'm just a humble chemist!"

"Yeah, right. Look, could you write that up for me and preserve the sample. I'll need some evidence if I'm going to make a fuss," Lyons said.

* * *

There was still no sign of life at the Faherty property, so they packed up all the gear. They replaced the cover on the well as best they could, and Loughran went back into the barn and put back the iron bar they had used to open up the cover.

They got back into the car and left, heading back to Mill Street.

When Lyons got back to the office, she decided to put a call through to Derivest. She looked up the website and wrote down the phone number on her jotter. Then, she dialled the number.

"Derivest Mining Corporation, how may I help you today?" the girl's voice at the other end of the line said.

"Oh, hello. I'm calling from Ireland. I wonder if I could speak to – hold on a second – Mr Jed Gilbert?"

"Just a moment – please stay on the line."

The phone cut over to some banal music, and Lyons expected to be put through to Mr Gilbert. The music went on for quite a few minutes, and Lyons couldn't help thinking of the cost of the call. Eventually, a new voice greeted her.

"Hi. This is Chuck Deri. I believe you're asking for Jed Gilbert."

"Yes, that's correct. My name is Inspector Maureen Lyons from the Irish police. I was hoping to have a word with him about your operation here in the west of Ireland."

"I see. Well, Jed isn't here just now. I'll see if I can contact him for you and get him to call you. Can I have your number?"

"Yes, of course." Lyons reeled off her number for the man. "But maybe you can tell me something about the work you have been doing here."

"No, I'm sorry. As far as I know we haven't got any exploration going on in Ireland at all at the moment. But that's Jed's baby. I'll get him to call you – OK?"

"Yes, thanks, Mr Deri. I look forward to hearing from him." By the time Lyons had spoken, the line had gone dead.

Chapter Thirteen

It was late in the afternoon when the phone on Lyons' desk sprang to life. The weather was closing in, and heavy grey clouds hung over the city, making it quite dark for the time of day. There was a storm forecast – the remnants of a hurricane that had battered the east coast of the USA and had then set off across the Atlantic to find Ireland. It was greatly reduced in power by now, but would still hold enough rain to cause localized flooding and make life miserable for the citizens of the city for a few days.

"Hello, Maureen, it's Séan."

"Oh, hi Séan, has the weather reached you there yet?"

"Ah, 'tis just starting. The wind is getting up something shocking and the rain won't be far behind. But look, I need a word. I had a call from that lassie up at the hotel, Nikola her name is. She told me that Jed Gilbert – you know that fella from the mining – is booked in again from tomorrow for a week."

"Is he now? That's very useful, Séan. I don't suppose she knows how he's getting here?"

"Well, I asked her that. She didn't know the details, but she said that she noticed he had a United MileagePlus tag on his suitcase last time he was here."

"Crikey, she should be a detective! That's great, because I was looking to speak to him and he was supposed to call me, but I haven't heard from him. I'll get onto the airline now and see when and where he's arriving. Thanks very much, Séan."

"No bother, Maureen. Let me know how you get on."

Lyons called John O'Connor into her office and asked him to contact United Airlines and find out what flight Gilbert was on, and if he was disembarking in Shannon or Dublin.

O'Connor was back in a few minutes.

"He's on the overnight from Newark. He's only booked as far as Shannon, so I guess that's where he's headed. Do you want me to alert the local boys at the airport?"

"No, John. That's OK. I'll look after it. What time does it land?"

"Hang on, I have it here somewhere. Here we are. It gets in at 5:20 a.m. or thereabouts – depending on the winds across the Atlantic."

"Lovely. Thanks, John."

When O'Connor had left, Lyons called Mick Hays.

"Hi, Mick, it's me. Listen, you don't fancy a drive down to Shannon Airport later on by any chance?"

"Maybe. What's on?"

Lyons explained about the arsenic that had been found in the water out at Faherty's farm, and that Loughran had told her that it could be related to core sampling by the mining company.

"And when I called the company in Utah, they were a bit evasive."

"OK. We can go soon if you like and we can book into the airport hotel. Say half an hour?"

"Yep! Fine. We can stop off at home and pick up toothbrushes. Give me a text when you're downstairs."

"Great. See you soon."

* * *

The drive from Galway to Shannon Airport should normally take just under an hour and a half. The new M18 motorway was a godsend, bypassing all the bottlenecks that had plagued motorists for years in the past. But with the weather getting ever worse, Mick Hays slowed down to take account of the reduced visibility and strong winds.

They arrived at soon after eight o'clock and checked in. The hotel was still able to provide an evening meal, and Hays and Lyons went straight to the dining room, both of them being ravenous after the journey.

When they were seated and being served, Hays opened the conversation.

"This is nice. I know it's work, but we haven't had a night away for a while."

"Don't get too excited, Mick. Remember we have to be up at four o'clock to meet the flight."

"I don't envy them on that one. They'll be blown all over the place in that wind."

"Ah, good enough for them! Anyway, what's new in your world?"

"It's a bit mad really. The pace of change in the force is picking up, and half the time you get the feeling that the main purpose of the Gardaí is being left behind. But Plunkett is on top of it. He brings the suits back to earth at every opportunity."

"What sort of things are going on?"

"Technology. The force is quite a bit behind our European counterparts, and we need to catch up," Hays said.

"What sort of things are coming?"

"There's an Automated Number-Plate Recognition roll-out coming right across the country. New fingerprint machines for mobile patrols, and ties to the computer systems used by Social Welfare, insurers, motor tax and joined up records across Europe for convictions."

"Wow, I see what you mean. That should make a lot of difference."

"Yes, it will, but I want to push it a bit further."

"As in?"

"Local DNA testing facilities to speed things up. Better forensic laboratories with more equipment and a complete overhaul of our communications."

"Great. Sinéad will love you forever. But isn't all that going to be very expensive?"

"That's the frustrating thing. The money isn't a problem. It's sitting there gathering dust. It's administration that are holding things back. They need a rocket up their arse. Speaking of which..."

Lyons glanced at her partner with a slightly concerned look.

"I called James McMahon yesterday. He said he hadn't forgotten about us. He has two candidate properties that he said would be reasonable value and are likely to appreciate nicely over the next few years."

"Oh, cool. And I was talking to our favourite bank manager too. After I fluttered my eyelashes at him, he was putty in my hand!"

"Are you serious?"

"No, not really, but I have to admit to flirting a little. But he's grand with it. He said as soon as we have identified the property we want to buy, to let him know, and he's put the process in motion."

"Nice. Let's see if we can get a viewing in later in the week."

The two finished their meal, which they both agreed was very good. They decided to get to bed as soon as possible, given the early start the following morning.

* * *

The United Airlines flight from Newark to Shannon was a miserable affair. Moderate to severe turbulence prevented any sleep, and the cabin crew were unable to serve drinks, although they did manage to get the evening meal delivered before it got too bad.

Jed Gilbert tried to rest on the lie-flat seat, but just couldn't manage it given the constant bouncing around and loud creaking from the machine as it sped through the storm.

The approach into Shannon was horrific. The pilots made their first approach with the plane crabbing wildly, and despite the windscreen wipers being set to their maximum speed, visibility was very poor. As they descended through 500 feet, the pilot called a go-around, and climbed the 767 back to 3,000 feet.

The second approach was a bit better. At 500 feet, the pilot called 'landing' and wrestled with the controls to line the plane up with the bright landing lights shining up through the lashing rain.

As the aircraft neared the runway, an automated warning in the cockpit sounded, 'glideslope, glideslope'. The captain ignored the warning and continued towards the airfield. As they crossed the threshold, a gust caught the plane and the left-hand wing dipped dangerously close to the tarmac. The pilot acted quickly, applying maximum opposite aileron to level the machine which finally touched down on the sodden ground with a heavy thud and the roar of reverse thrust. Thirty seconds later the plane had slowed to 30 Kph, and the crew turned off the runway and taxied towards the terminal.

The plane finally docked and the bleary-eyed passengers started to retrieve their luggage and coats from the overhead bins and make their way into the building. Business class passengers were disembarked first, and it wasn't long before Jed Gilbert was walking along the familiar corridors towards the baggage collection area.

Chapter Fourteen

Inside the terminal, the strong wind could be heard gusting around the cavernous shell of the building. Lyons and Hays were standing outside arrivals, and soon Lyons spotted a man holding a card in front of him with 'Mr Gilbert' written in thick black marker on it. She strolled over to where he was standing.

"Good morning. Are you waiting for Mr Jed Gilbert from Derivest?" she said.

"Yes, that's right. I hope he made the flight. It's too bloody early for me to be up at this hour on a wild goose chase," the man said, and added, "why? Who wants to know?"

"I am waiting for him too. I just need a few words before you whisk him off. Where is he going anyway?"

"Bloody Clifden. It will take me hours to get there and back in this weather. Still, I suppose it's not a bad fare at this time of the year."

"Does he often come through here on his way to the west?"

"Every few weeks. We have the Derivest account, so I suppose in a few days I'll be trekking back up to bloody Connemara to fetch him."

"Oh, right. What company do you drive for?" Lyons said.

"Sarsfield Car and Bus Hire. We have a pretty big fleet these days, but I always seem to draw the early morning pick-ups. Must be something I said to the boss, or his wife."

Lyons was in no doubt that this man's grumpy demeanour hadn't won him any popularity competition with his employer.

"Ah well, never mind. The weather is due to pick up later. It'll be a grand drive back."

Just then the passengers started coming through from the Newark flight, so Lyons paid attention. Gilbert was the tenth person to arrive. He walked over to the man holding the card.

"Morning, Liam. Thanks for collecting me."

Lyons stepped in.

"Mr Gilbert, my name is Inspector Maureen Lyons from the Galway police. I wonder if we could have a few words before you set off with Liam here?"

Gilbert looked surprised.

"I guess. But we can't keep Liam waiting too long, and I'm feeling exhausted. I didn't sleep a wink on the flight. It was bouncing all over the place all night."

Lyons turned to the driver.

"Why don't you go and get yourself a cup of tea, Liam. We'll only be a few minutes."

Liam wasn't happy, but he didn't want any issue with the Gardaí either, so he did as Lyons suggested.

"I'd like to introduce Superintendent Michael Hays, Mr Gilbert. Let's sit over here where it's a bit quieter."

Hays shook hands with Gilbert, and the three of them made their way over to the side of the building where there was a row of seats and a few small round tables.

"Can I get you a coffee, Mr Gilbert?" Hays said.

"No thanks. That will only keep me awake. I intend to sleep all the way," he said, smiling. "How can I help you folks anyway?"

"We understand your company – Derivest – is interested in exploring for minerals in the area east of Clifden, close to the coast. Is that correct?"

"Yes, that's right. But it's still at a very early stage. It looks promising though. There could be some significant deposits of metals under the bog there."

"So have you been taking core samples and the like?" Hays asked.

"Yes. We have. We've sampled several areas. The material is sent to a lab in the UK for analysis, and so far, the results have been quite promising."

"Would the work you have been doing have disturbed the ground much, or affected the water table in any way?" Lyons asked.

"Oh, gee, no. We use a two-inch bore drill that goes down about twenty or thirty feet into the soil, or rock mostly in those parts, but the impact on the ground is miniscule. There wouldn't be any disturbance. Why do you ask?"

"Have you come across two brothers that live in that area – at Boolagare – the Fahertys?"

"Yes, I have as it happens. I've met them both. Very different, the two of them. But why the interest in our activities, Inspector? Is anything wrong?"

Lyons looked to Hays for guidance, and he nodded imperceptibly.

"Yes, there is, Mr Gilbert. Young Davin Faherty was found dead in one of the streams near Shannalecka Lough. He appears to have ingested arsenic."

"God, that's awful. Is foul play suspected?"

"We're still investigating, Mr Gilbert. Tell me, did your company find any traces of arsenic in the water out there or in the soil?" Hays said.

"Yes, yes we did. It's one of the indicators for copper and even gold. It's what first put us on to the idea that we might have a workable claim. But nothing that we did would have caused the arsenic to get into someone's body – that's impossible."

"How is your claim going anyway?" Lyons said.

"Oh, you know. These things take an age to sort out. There are any number of hoops that we have to jump through, and lots of different authorities that we have to satisfy, not to mention the locals. It's a very slow process."

"Have you encountered much resistance?" Hays said.

"We always encounter resistance, Superintendent. But our efforts can also bring significant prosperity into an area. And let's face it, that place isn't exactly a hive of industry just now. If we do go ahead, and I say 'if', there could be plenty of jobs and money coming into the hotels, shops and pubs. It could do a lot for the entire west of Connemara."

"And what about the disruption to the landscape, the machinery, the noise, the wildlife?" Lyons said.

"Look, Inspector, I don't have the time right now, and in any case I'm not in the humour, to take you through our complete environmental pack, but I'd be happy to do so at some stage. I can promise you, Derivest maintains the highest possible standards in that regard. We always strive to leave a place in better condition than it was when we went there, and let's face it, that won't be hard in this case. Now, if you'll excuse me, my driver is getting impatient."

Gilbert stood up and made it clear that, as far as he was concerned, their discussion was over. As he prepared to leave, Lyons asked, "How long will you be in Ireland this time, Mr Gilbert?"

"About a week – no more," he said rather curtly.

"And will you be staying at the Alcock and Brown for the entire length of your stay?"

"My, you have been doing your homework, haven't you? Yes, Inspector, I will. Now if you'll excuse me, I have a cab to catch."

* * *

Outside in the car park, Hays and Lyons discussed their early morning meeting with the man from Derivest.

"What did you make of our Mr Gilbert?" Lyons said.

"Even making allowances for the fact that he was just off an uncomfortable flight, I didn't like him," Hays said.

"Anything specific?"

"No. Just a feeling I got. I think he was relieved that we didn't probe him further. But I can tell you, I'm not finished with Mr Jed Gilbert yet. Tell you what, most likely he'll go for a sleep when he gets to Clifden. Then, later on when he's rested, he'll be in the hotel bar. You know how these Americans like to talk. Why don't we plant someone in the bar and see if they can chat him up?" Hays said.

"Really, Superintendent, you can be very devious at times. One of Seán's men?"

"No. No, I was thinking more of someone like Mary Fallon – you know, pretty blonde, young, attractive. In civvies of course."

"You mean a full-on honeytrap! Jesus!" Lyons said.

"She doesn't have to sleep with the guy, just have a nice long chat about himself, his work and his company over a few drinks – strong ones."

"Hmm, I suppose. Shall I give Roundstone a call when the hour gets decent and set it up?"

"Yes, do please. Now let's get out of here. I haven't finished sleeping myself yet."

Chapter Fifteen

Sally Fahy sat down in the threadbare armchair that she had placed in the window of the empty house at the Newcastle Road crossroads. It was just after eight o'clock, and she was anticipating a long night. Her colleague, one Philip Dewar, had been allocated to her by Liam O'Higgins and was seated uncomfortably on a hard wooden chair that he had retrieved from downstairs. Dewar was a rather serious young Garda. He had been in the drug squad for over a year, and O'Higgins had reported that he was a useful member of the team, as he could infiltrate some of the less well organised groups that ply their evil trade in the city with ease. That would only last so long though. They would get to know him eventually, and then he'd have to be moved to another region to protect his safety.

"So, Philip, tell me about yourself," Fahy said, taking a sip from the can of Diet Coke she had brought with her.

"There's not much to tell. I'm originally from Dublin, though my parents are from Sligo. I joined the Guards after school and after a year on the beat around Dublin, I applied for the drug squad. They were recruiting at the time. But I'm glad to be out of there. The drug crowd in Dublin are animals. They'd slit you quick as look at you."

"Ah, don't worry, Philip, we have a few nasty types out here in the west that would take pleasure is seeing you off just as handy. But don't worry, I'll look after ye," Fahy said, smiling, but she noticed that Dewar remained straight-faced.

"So, what's the story here then, Sergeant?" he said after a few minutes of awkward silence.

"Well, that little cottage over there is a grow house. Some bloke comes along each night, I presume to check the CO_2 levels and see that the lamps are still all working and do whatever else is required, so we are here to see what we can find out."

"Are we supposed to grab him? What if he's armed?"

"Nothing so dramatic, Philip. Our guys have their eye on the people further up the food chain. This fella is just a lacky. So we are to see if we can follow him and find out a bit more about him. That's all. No heroics."

"I see. Does he arrive on foot?" Dewar said.

"Yes, he does. But he may have a car parked in another street. He's pretty cautious."

The same uneasy silence descended on the two of them.

* * *

It was after ten by the time there was any action at the little house. Some light mist had descended on the area, brought down by temperature inversion and a lot of moisture in the air, and for once, the wind was calm.

Sally was first to spot the shadowy figure of the young man approaching the property. Once again, he did a circuit of the place, observing to make sure that there was no one about. He looked in all the parked cars, and when he was satisfied that he was not being observed, he went around the back of the cottage and disappeared.

"Here we go," Fahy said, "he's gone inside."

"Right. What do you want to do?"

"Let's get out on the street. If he follows the usual pattern, he'll be in there for half an hour or so, but I don't want to take any chances. Let's go."

As they made their way out onto the cold damp footpath, Fahy said, "We may have to make it look like we're a couple out for a walk. If he comes out, put your arm around me, OK?"

Philip Dewar wasn't entirely happy about that idea. It wasn't that Sally Fahy wasn't a good-looking girl – she was, very much so – but Dewar had visions of a sexual harassment claim being brought against him. He wasn't quite used to the ways of the Galway Gardaí as yet.

The two Gardaí waited in the shadows at the front of the pharmacy, keeping a close eye on the grow house using the reflection in the chemist's shop window. After about twenty minutes, the hooded man emerged from the side of the house and turned to go back down the road in the direction from which he had come.

"Put your arm around me, Philip," Fahy whispered, and the young Garda obeyed.

The man from the grow house was walking quickly, and they found it quite difficult to keep up with him without breaking into a run. Luckily, both Dewar and Fahy had rubber-soled shoes, so they made little noise as they pursued their quarry through the mist.

The road ended in a T-junction, and by the time Fahy and Dewar got to the intersection, there was no sign of their man. They peered through the thickening gloom left and right, but could see nothing. Fearing that they had been spotted, and that the man was still watching them, Fahy leant into Dewar as if to embrace him, without their faces actually meeting. Then she pushed him away, and said "Goodnight love," loudly. Dewar took the hint and replied, before the two of them set off in opposite directions in the hope of picking up the trail again.

Fahy had turned into New Road, and was walking back towards the city, but there was no sign of anyone. On her own now, she could walk more quickly, and with determination, head down looking at the path, but ever watchful for anyone hiding in any of the gardens or up any of the small alleys.

After ten minutes, when she had reached the river, she decided to turn back. It was no use; they had lost him. She texted Dewar on her mobile phone.

"Anything?"

"No. Meet back at the junction."

Dewar's journey had taken him down a narrow street with cars parked on either side, despite the double yellow lines all along the kerb, and lights on in the small terraced houses on both sides. As he neared the junction again, keeping a sharp eye out for the miscreant, a vehicle suddenly burst into life and sped past him going much too quickly for the conditions. It rounded the corner at the end of the road ignoring the stop sign, and was gone.

* * *

"Did you get a good look at it?" Fahy asked when they were back together again.

"No, sorry. It all happened too fast, and there was a lot of exhaust smoke too, so I couldn't see it properly."

"Fuck it! Never mind. What colour was it anyway?"

"Dunno – something dark, I think."

"Did you even get the make?"

"It was a jeep of some kind. I'm not much good with cars."

"Have you called it in?" Fahy said.

"Eh, no. I didn't think."

Fahy said nothing but immediately got on her radio.

"Be on the lookout for a dark-coloured jeep being driven recklessly in the Newcastle Road area. Registration unknown. Driver is a person of interest."

Her call was acknowledged, and the word went out.

As the two Gardaí made their way back to where their own cars were parked, Fahy called Maureen Lyons on her mobile.

"Hi, boss. It's Sally. Sorry to call so late. I was wondering if there was any chance of calling in for a minute?"

"Yes, sure, Sally. We're not in bed yet. What's up?" Lyons said.

"I'll tell you when I see you. I'll be about fifteen minutes, if that's OK?"

"Yes, sure. See you then."

* * *

"Come in, Sally. Can I get you anything?" Maureen said, letting Fahy into the sitting room. Hays was sitting on the sofa reading a magazine, so the two women went into the kitchen.

"Thanks, boss. I could murder a cup of coffee, if you'll pardon the expression!"

"That good, is it?" Lyons said.

"God, give me strength. I thought the drug squad were supposed to be elite. Don't get me started."

Fahy went on to relate the events of the evening to Lyons.

"I'm not looking forward to telling O'Higgins. I don't want to land Dewar right in it, but it was pretty amateur. Any ideas?" Fahy said.

"Yes. I have. Why don't you let me talk to Liam? I can put some kind of a gloss over it while at the same time making sure he knows it wasn't your fault. Do you think me laddo is on to us?"

"Actually, no. I think he was just keen to get away from the place. I doubt if he copped Dewar or myself. We looked just like an ordinary couple out for a walk."

"I hope you were gentle with him, Sally," Lyons said with a smirk.

"Oh, for fuck sake, boss. Have you seen him? He's a lanky streak of misery – not my type at all."

"That's what you say! Anyway, what are you going to do next about this grow house?" Lyons said.

"That's up to O'Higgins. I'd say they'd have to move in on it now and take their chances. There's probably quite a bit of forensic in the house. These lads can only be so careful."

"Do you want to get out of it? I can tell O'Higgins we can't spare you anymore if you like – bigger fish to fry and all that," Lyons said.

"No. Let's see what they want to do next, but much appreciated all the same. God, I feel better with a hot drink inside me. It was bloody freezing in that place."

Chapter Sixteen

When Lyons got to work the following day, there were two reports on her desk from forensics. One was the full post-mortem result on Davin Faherty, the other was from Sinéad Loughran concerning what they had found in the Land Rover belonging to Davin's brother.

Lyons read both with interest, and then called her team together in the open plan.

"Right, folks. Let's see what we have so far."

She went through the evidence, such as it was.

"We know Davin died from arsenic poisoning. The water from the well on their property has been analysed, and while there are some very slight traces of arsenic, it's not nearly enough to have caused either of them serious harm. In any case, the other brother is still alive and well, so we can assume that Davin didn't die from the drinking water. The working assumption must be that he was deliberately poisoned."

"But why, boss?" Eamon Flynn asked.

"That's what we need to find out, Eamon. Let's look at who gains from his death."

"No one, as far as I can see," Flynn said.

"Well, maybe, or maybe not. There's the brother for starters. He presumably now owns the whole lot out there, for what it's worth," Lyons said.

"Not much, boss. Would you like to be the proud owner of a few acres of bog and rock miles from anywhere?" Fahy said.

"A few acres of bog and rock that could have copper and gold in it, Sally. Puts a bit of a different slant on it, don't you think?"

"Hmm. Maybe. But still, if there's a decent haul there would be enough for both of them, surely?" Fahy said.

"Don't underestimate greed as a motive for murder, Sally. I've seen it before. It's not nice. But listen, we need to find out if there's any possible connection with the mining company and these events. Did we set up Mary Fallon to do a bit of work on Gilbert?"

"Yes, boss. She was a bit uneasy about it. Not what we asked her to do, but she wasn't sure if she could carry it off."

"Ah, don't worry. Mary Fallon has talents that she doesn't even know she possesses – trust me, I've seen her in action," Lyons said.

A muted laugh went around the room.

"Anything from forensics on Laughlin's Land Rover, boss?" Flynn asked.

"Oh, yes, I nearly forgot. They gave it a good going-over. There's all sorts of crap all over it. Lots of traces of Davin too – fingerprints, DNA, and other stuff. But nothing conclusive. Nothing to say that he was carried in the back, post-mortem at least."

"Terrific. What about the black plastic he was wrapped in?" Flynn said.

"Good point, Eamon. I hadn't thought of that. I'll get onto Sinéad again and see if there is anything. OK, jobs for today. Eamon, can you dig deep into this guy Jed Gilbert? See what you can find on him. I get the impression he's a bit slippery. Find out where he's coming from, and don't worry if you stir up a bit of a hornet's nest. He's been spending too much time in Clifden for my liking. Sally, can you see if you can dig up a bit more on Davin Faherty – you know, known associates, anything from his past that might have pissed someone off, mobile phone records, that sort of thing?"

"Sure, boss. What are you going to do?"

"Me? I'm going to mercilessly exploit my relationship with the Superintendent to turn over a few stones – see if there are any creepy-crawlies to be found! But first, a word in my office, Sally."

Fahy thought she might be in some kind of trouble with Lyons. It would be unusual – the two of them worked well together normally. She followed Lyons into her office, feeling a little anxious.

"I just wanted to find out if traffic came up with anything on the car that made off at the grow house last night, Sally?"

"Oh, right. No. 'fraid not. They didn't come across it anywhere but it was fairly misty afterwards, so I'm not really surprised. I'm not convinced that we were actually spotted by the guy. I think he just wanted to get away from the place as quickly as he could."

"OK. I'll speak to Liam later on and see what he wants to do now. Thanks, Sally."

* * *

Hays was in his office, and was glad of the interruption when Lyons asked to see him. He'd been toiling over a report that the Superintendent had asked him to prepare on 'Inter-regional co-operation in An Garda Síochána', which to Hays was a bit of a joke, but apparently someone was going to make their career on the basis of it.

"Hi, come in. How's things?" Hays said.

"Ah, ye know – so-so. What about you?"

"Much the same. Anyway, nice to see you. Maybe you can distract me from this effing report," he said with a slightly sly smile.

"Now, now, Superintendent, behave."

"Damn! Anyway, what's on your mind?"

"I was hoping you might be able to do a bit of detecting for me. You know we are investigating that business out at Shannalecka – the young guy that was killed – well there's possibly some kind of connection to a US mining company – Derivest. I was wondering if you could use your vast network of contacts to find out a bit about them?"

"Hmm. OK. What sort of information are you after?" Hays said.

"I'm not entirely sure to be honest. Just wondering if they are more or less trustworthy – if they have treated the areas where they mine for copper and gold sympathetically, and how they have handled the locals, that sort of thing."

"OK. Do you think there's a connection?"

Lyons reminded Hays about the arsenic found in Davin's body, and the traces in the well water.

"A bit tenuous, don't you think?"

"Maybe. That's what I'm hoping to find out. It would be of particular interest if there had been any funny business involving them when they were trying to stake a claim. And I'd love to know about their interaction with the locals here too. That Gilbert guy has been around a lot this summer, and he may have been getting up to something. Do you think you could get the low-down for me?"

"I'll give it my best. I think it's a bit of a long shot, but I know better than to go against the famous Lyons instinct!"

"That's the spirit, Superintendent. How nice it is to have an obliging senior officer at my beck and call."

"Watch it, Lyons! I hear they are recruiting in West Kerry. Nice place – in the summer," Hays said.

They both got up and put away the banter. Hays came round to where Lyons was standing and gave her a warm hug and a kiss. She snuggled into him for a few moments, enjoying the warmth and bulk of his sturdy frame.

"Much as I'd like to continue, Maureen, I'd better get on. The boss will be on my case if I haven't got this drafted soon."

"OK, love. Catch you later."

* * *

When Lyons had left, Hays thought for a few minutes about the best way to find out about Derivest without being obvious. Then, he had an idea.

"Hi, James, it's Mick Hays here. How are you?"

"Oh hello, Mick. Good, thanks – but busy. What can I do for you?"

"Sorry to disturb you, James. I was wondering if you knew anything about that mineral exploration thing that's going on out near Clifden – you know the one that this American crowd, Derivest, are into?"

"Oh, yes. I do as it happens. We've been doing some work with them. They wanted drawings of a few buildings that they hope to erect out there, and they also looked for some before and after landscape pictures that they could use to keep the natives quiet. A bit out of the norm for us to be honest, but they pay well," McMahon said.

"I see. And how are the natives, as you call them, taking all this?"

"It's mixed. The traders in Clifden are licking their lips. It would mean a real shot in the arm for them if Derivest actually found anything. They could be there for years gently extracting ore and doing a bit of processing. But then there's the local farmers. They're not so happy at all. Even if the mining company bought up some land, they still think in the old ways, you know."

"And have Derivest made any suggestions about the general infrastructure out there – you know, the roads in particular?" Hays said.

"Yes, they have. They've been working with the Council to see if they could get the N59 upgraded – widened and flattened a bit. And they'll need a better access road to the harbour too. They have some idea about bringing a ship into Clifden harbour to take away the ore, so they've been talking to the Harbour Commission about building some kind of a long gantry out into the sea to carry the stuff to where the ships could anchor. I've seen something like it on the North Wales coast near Conwy. It works pretty well."

"Hmm, they're pretty serious about this then. They must be expecting significant deposits too?"

"Yes, they are. I was out there during the summer and I got talking to one of their geologists – a guy from Norway – nice chap, if a bit serious. He said there might be significant deposits of minerals there. Well worth investigating further. But he told me to keep quiet about it. They didn't want the word to get out," McMahon said.

"Is there anyone in particular in the Council that might be worth talking to?"

"The main contact is a guy called Ronnie Wilkinson. I know him pretty well. He's OK, mostly."

"That's great, James. Would it be OK to contact him, do you think?"

"Yes, sure. He's very approachable."

"Great. Just one more thing. Were there any particular local people – maybe farmers – who were particularly vocal in their opposition to the whole thing, James?"

"I couldn't say, Mick. But your folks from Clifden should have a handle on that, surely?"

"Yes, good point. Listen, that's all very interesting, James. Many thanks. I'll let you get back to work. We must meet for lunch one of the days."

"Yes, definitely. Give me a call in about a week. Thanks, Mick."

Hays put a call through to the Council offices to speak to Ronnie Wilkinson, but the man was out on a site inspection. Hays left a message for him to call him back, but didn't mention that he was from the Garda.

Chapter Seventeen

Mary Fallon was getting ready for her night out. She was trying to figure out what the most appropriate outfit would be, although in fairness it wasn't that difficult. She had a pair of very expensive and beautifully tailored blue denim jeans, and she selected a shoe-string top in shiny pink satin, and a leather bomber jacket.

"That should do the trick," she said, applying a dab of perfume behind her ears and on the underside of her wrists. She tied her shoulder-length blonde hair back in a pony tail, and completed her ensemble with the small gold watch that her parents had given her for her twenty-first birthday.

When Mary arrived at the bar in the Alcock and Brown Hotel, it was pretty empty. She sat up to the counter and climbed onto a bar stool and ordered a vodka and tonic with ice and a slice from Áine, the barmaid, whom she knew a little from previous nights out with her mates.

When the drink was served, Mary said, "Áine. Listen. I'll be ordering a few more drinks here, but I don't want any more vodka. Just make it look real for me, will you?"

The barmaid was a bit puzzled, but was happy to oblige. She would still charge for the spirit, and put the proceeds in her purse while serving Mary water and lime cordial.

It wasn't long before Jed Gilbert took the bait. He had been sitting in an armchair beside the open turf fire, and when his glass was empty, he stood up and approached the bar close to where Mary was seated.

Pouring a pint of Guinness is a well-practiced art. You don't simply fill the glass with the dark brown liquid. Rather, the glass is tilted against the tap, and filled to two-thirds, and then left to settle for two or three minutes. Once the bubbles in the stout have formed a creamy head on the drink, and the remainder is black, the drink is topped off and left to settle for a final minute, so that the customer gets a pint of dark liquid with a pale beige creamy top, about three-quarters of an inch deep. The drinker observes this ritual closely, using the time to build up his or her anticipation of the pleasure to come – and of course allowing time for conversation with pretty blonde girls at the bar.

"Hi. Can I get you a refill?" Jed asked Mary.

"Thank you. That would be very nice," Mary responded, turning and smiling at the man.

Gilbert nodded to Áine, who got the message and turned her back on the two of them while she prepared Mary's harmless glass of water.

"So, are you on your own this evening?" Gilbert said.

"I'm waiting for a few friends, but I'm a bit early. Time is kind of approximate in Clifden. But do I detect an American accent?"

"Yes, that's right. I'm Jed Gilbert, and I'm from Utah," Gilbert said, extending his hand.

"Mary Fallon, from Clifden," Fallon said, shaking his hand and smiling at him.

"Nice to meet you, Mary. Do you mind if I keep you company while you're waiting for your friends?"

"No, of course not. And thanks for the drink. So, tell me, Jed, what has you here in Clifden at this time of the year? There's not much going on."

"Oh, I'm here on business. Very boring. But I enjoy the place. What do you do?" Gilbert asked.

"I'm at college in Galway, but I get back home as often as I can to meet the girls."

"What are you studying?"

"Just a general arts degree. I'm not very clever," Fallon said.

"Never mind. You're very pretty. That will take you further than your degree in life – trust me, I know about these things."

Fallon managed to blush a little at the compliment, and looked down at the floor as if embarrassed.

"What sort of business are you in, Jed?"

"Mining. I work for an exploration company in the States. We mine copper and other metals."

"Wow! Sounds exciting. But surely there's none of that stuff out here. It's all bog and rocks as far as I can see."

"It's deep in the ground – under the bog and rocks. And as it happens, we think there's quite a bit of it here."

"Really! That's cool. Have you started digging it out yet?"

"No. Not yet. Maybe next summer if we can get the necessary permits arranged."

"Sounds really interesting. I never imagined that there would be anything like that going on in little old Clifden. But tell me, Jed, what about you? Are you married?" Fallon said, leaning in a little closer to the man so that he could see a little of her cleavage.

"Nah. I was once, but this job isn't good for a marriage. I'm away nearly all the time, and she got fed up with it."

"Sorry to hear that. Look, you'll have to excuse me for a minute – I need the bathroom," Fallon said, holding onto Gilbert's arm to steady herself as she climbed down from the high stool.

He reached out and helped her down, and they came very close as she landed on the floor, so that Gilbert got a waft of her perfume.

Mary had left her handbag over the back of a chair beside where she was seated. When she had left the room, Gilbert peered into it, and spotted her warrant card sticking up out of an inside pocket.

When Mary returned, the lounge in the hotel was starting to fill up. Áine was busy serving the various tables that were now occupied.

"Why don't we sit over at the fire, Mary?" Gilbert said. "Bring your drink."

When they sat down, Gilbert observed that none of Mary's friends seemed to have turned up.

"I might have got the time wrong. I'm always doing that. They'll be here soon. So, what's life in Utah like, Jed?"

"Utah is mostly mountains, so it's very hot in summer and very cold in winter. But it's a nice place for most of the time. People are friendly, and we have everything we need in Logan – that's the city where the company is based."

"Have you always worked for Derivest?"

Gilbert hadn't told the girl the name of the company that he was working for, so his senses were suddenly fully alert to what was going on.

"Just a few years now. They're a pretty good outfit – very flexible. But look, your glass is almost empty – let me get you a top-up."

"I shouldn't really – I've had three already. And you can't buy me drink all night – it's not fair. Can I get you one?" Fallon said.

"Not at all. I'm on expenses," he said, tapping the side of his nose.

Mary smiled, and Gilbert stood up and went to the bar for another vodka and lime which Áine produced using the arrangement she had made earlier.

Another hour went by, with Mary trying, unsuccessfully, to pump Gilbert for information about himself, with little result. She learned that he had two children from his original marriage, and that they were teenagers, but very little else. She tried to get him to talk more about his career, but he wasn't having any. Eventually, Mary got fed up and decided to leave.

"Well, it looks as if my friends have deserted me altogether. I think I'll just head home, Jed. It was really nice meeting you," she said, gathering her bag and jacket and getting up to leave. 'Strange,' she said to herself, 'I've been drinking water all evening, but I feel very light-headed.'

"Here, let me walk you home, Mary. I think you're a bit unsteady on your feet," Gilbert said.

"I'm OK, really," she replied, feeling anything but.

"No, I insist. Do you live far?"

"No, just down to the bottom of the street and then a little bit further in to the left."

"OK. Let's go."

As soon as Mary hit the fresh air, the drug that Gilbert had slipped into her drink while she was at the toilet hit her hard. She stumbled, and Jed had to act quickly to stop her having a fall. He supported her weight, and led her down along Market Street towards her flat.

* * *

It was nearly ten o'clock the next day when Pascal Brosnan decided he had better do something about his colleague, Mary Fallon. She hadn't turned up for work in the Garda station on the edge of Roundstone village, which was totally unheard of in her case. She was, normally, totally reliable.

Brosnan tried her mobile number again, but it went straight through to voicemail. He didn't bother to leave a message this time – there were already three in her phone from earlier. Somewhat reluctantly, for he didn't want to get Mary into trouble, he put a call through to Maureen Lyons in Galway.

"Hi, Pascal, what's up?" Lyons said, recognising the number on her mobile phone.

"Hello, Inspector. I was just wondering if you knew anything about Mary's whereabouts? She hasn't appeared for work this morning, and it's most unlike her. I'm a bit concerned."

"Oh, I see. When did you last hear from her, Pascal?"

"Yesterday when she was going off duty at just after five. She said she wanted to get away promptly – she was meeting someone, but I don't know who."

"Hmmm... that's right. Look, Pascal, Mary was doing a little job for us last night. She was meeting up with a Mr Jed Gilbert at the Alcock and Brown. But she didn't call in after the meeting. Maybe she got lucky!"

"Mary's not like that, Inspector – not at all. She wouldn't go off with a stranger. What did you say this fella's name was?"

"Gilbert – Jed Gilbert. He's an American."

"Right, well I'm going to go out to Clifden and see what I can find. I'll call to Mary's place first, and if I can't raise her, I'll go and have a word with your Mr Gilbert. I'll let you know what I find out. OK?"

"Do you not think it might be better to let one of Séan's men go around to see if she's still at home, Pascal?"

"No, Inspector, I don't. She's my responsibility. I'll deal with it."

Lyons could tell there was no point in trying to persuade Pascal Brosnan to do anything other than what he had planned. She had long thought that there was more to their relationship than just work, but she had no basis, other than her powerful instinct, for thinking that.

"OK, Pascal. Please keep me informed."

"I will, Inspector, don't worry."

Lyons could tell from Brosnan's tone that he felt Lyons was in some way responsible for what may have happened to Mary Fallon, and he was angry. She wondered whether she should contact Séan Mulholland herself, and put him in the picture, but decided against it. That would only cause more issues with Brosnan, which she didn't want.

* * *

Mary Fallon awoke just before ten o'clock. She felt dreadful. She had an awful headache, and when she tried to get up, she was dizzy and had to sit down again quickly on the edge of the bed to stop herself from falling over.

"Christ, what the hell happened to me?" she said to herself, holding her sore head in both hands. She looked down. At least she was still fully dressed, but her mouth felt like it was full of sand, and her co-ordination was all over the place. She tried to stand up again, this time with more success. She staggered into the bathroom and looked in the mirror. Her hair was a mess, and there were black circles under her eyes, but apart from that, she seemed to be more or less intact.

She then went back into the kitchen-living room and located some soluble paracetamol, and set it to dissolve in a glass of cold water.

God, I must phone Pascal – he'll be worried sick, she thought. She located her phone in her clutch bag and dialled Roundstone Garda. The message informed her that the station was unmanned at the moment, and if the caller had an emergency, they should either call Clifden Gardaí or 999. She then went and drank down the fizzy liquid to see if she could somehow dispel the pounding in her head.

Mary was just finishing the remedy when her doorbell rang. She got up and went to the door and found Pascal Brosnan outside with a worried look on his face.

"Jesus, Mary, thank God you're OK. Can I come in?"

"Hi, Pascal, yes of course. I'm OK — but not in very good shape. You couldn't put on some strong coffee for me, could you?"

"Yes, of course. What happened?"

"I wish I knew. I met up with this Yank to see if I could get some information from him about the mining caper out at Boolagare. I was only drinking water — but when I went to go home, I kinda blacked out. It's never happened to me before. The last thing I remember is him propping me up on the footpath outside the hotel — and then nothing, till I woke up here this morning with a thundering headache feeling like shit."

"Christ. Has that ever happened to you before?" Brosnan said.

"No, course not. I don't understand it at all. Look, can you hang on here for a few minutes. I need to shower and change, then we'd better get into work."

"Yeah, sure. But, Mary, can I make a suggestion?"

"Course."

"Any chance you could save a urine sample for analysis. It sounds like you've been drugged to me."

"Just what every female Garda hopes for, Pascal — her colleague asking her to keep some pee! Yeah, I suppose so, that's not a bad idea. It's the only explanation I can come up with. But why?"

"Well, he must have helped you home. Can you tell if the place has been gone over? Or did he just root in your handbag?"

"I dunno. I haven't time for all this now, anyway, let me just get into the shower and then let's go."

"OK. Here's your coffee then," he said, handing her a mug of steaming, strong black coffee.

Chapter Eighteen

Pascal Brosnan called Lyons while Mary Fallon was in the shower. He told her what he believed had happened to Mary on her night out with Gilbert.

"OK, Pascal. I'm going to call Séan and have him send someone up to the hotel to have a word with Gilbert. That was quick thinking about the sample. I'll call Sinéad and see how she wants to have it processed. I'm not sure if we'll find anything, but you never know. Give me a call when you get to Roundstone. And look after Mary for us, won't you?"

"I certainly will, Inspector. Are you sure you don't want me to go and talk to this Gilbert fella?"

"No, Pascal, better not. You might lamp him one! Séan will probably send Jim Dolan up. We don't want to cause an international incident with Gilbert – not yet anyway."

"OK. Probably best. I'll give you a ring in about half an hour then."

Fallon emerged from the bathroom wrapped in a fluffy pink towelling robe. She looked a lot better, and Pascal told her so.

"Thanks, Pascal. Just give me a few minutes to dry my hair and put on my work clothes," she said, heading for the bedroom.

Fifteen minutes later they were in Brosnan's car on the way back into Roundstone.

* * *

Jim Dolan had been briefed by Séan Mulholland following Lyons' call. He wasted no time in driving up to the Alcock and Brown to see Jed Gilbert.

"Hi, Nikola," Dolan said to the receptionist.

"Oh, hello, officer. How can I help you today?"

"I'm looking for one of your residents – a Mr Jed Gilbert. Is he about?"

"No, he's not. He checked out early this morning. It's funny, because he was booked in for another two nights."

"Did he leave a forwarding address, or say where he was going?"

"No, but we have an address for his company. Do you want it?" the girl said.

"Yes, please, thanks."

Nikola wrote out the address for Derivest in Logan, Utah on a Post-it note and handed it to Dolan.

On the way back to the station, Dolan called Lyons.

"Yer man has done a bunk, boss. He checked out a few days early, so I guess he may be on his way back to the States."

"OK, thanks, Jim. I'll get John to check with United Airlines and see if he's made a booking. But my guess is, if he has been up to no good, that he might go to the UK first. But we definitely need to speak to him. He's now a person of interest with regard to the Faherty case. And I'm not having some Yank messing around with one of ours and getting away with it."

"Right, boss. Do you need me to do any more?"

"No, thanks, Jim. Just write it up with the timings and email it to me. Cheers."

* * *

Brosnan and Fallon set off along the old bog road from Clifden to Roundstone. It was a nice morning, and when they got to Ballyconneely where the road ran along the coast, the sun came out and danced on the bright blue waves of the Atlantic Ocean. The heathland looked splendid, the purple heather contrasting with the green of the reeds, and the blue of the Twelve Pins in the background. But their minds were on other things.

"How could I have been such a fool? I even made arrangements for the barmaid to top me up with water instead of vodka every time I had another drink. He must have slipped something into it when he was up at the bar."

"Don't beat yourself up, Mary. It looks to me as if he is an experienced bloke who has done this kind of thing before. I wonder what put him onto you?" Brosnan said.

"Maybe nothing. He might just have wanted to check me out – you know, just being suspicious of a girl on her own in Clifden allowing herself to be chatted up like that. But Inspector Lyons will be livid. I feel such an idiot."

"Actually, I don't think she will. After all, thanks to you, we've flushed him out."

"Yeah, but if he gets away to the States, that'll be the end of it. We'll never get him back, even if he is guilty of murder."

Just then, Brosnan's phone rang, and he answered it using the Bluetooth device in the car.

"Hi, Pascal. It's Maureen Lyons here. I just wanted to let you know that Sinéad is sending someone out to collect Mary's sample. They should be with you shortly. We'll have it analysed immediately and then we should be able to get a warrant for Gilbert – if we can find him. Is Mary there with you?"

"Yes, she's here."

"Hello, Inspector."

"Mary, did Gilbert give any hint about where he was heading next?"

"No, boss. To be honest it was very difficult to get him to give up any personal details at all. I thought he would be all gab but I had to work hard to get anything out of him. I think that's what might have put him on to me. I'm sorry, boss."

"Don't apologise, Mary. You did OK. How are you feeling?"

"Still a bit groggy, to be honest, but I'm fine."

"Pascal, be sure to look after Mary today, won't you? OK. I have to go now. Let me know if there are any developments."

When Lyons had finished the call, she spoke to John O'Connor and asked him to contact the airlines.

"Not just United, John, get onto the local airlines too. He may have decided to go to London first to take a less obvious route home. And don't forget Belfast."

"Righto, boss."

"And ask Eamon to come in, would you?"

"Yes, sure."

A moment later, Eamon Flynn came into Lyons' office.

"Hi, Eamon. What did you get on Jed Gilbert?"

"I've not quite finished burrowing yet but he's an interesting character. He hasn't been with Derivest all that long. And he didn't always live in Utah either. He had a charge under federal law for crimes against a person in Florida, but the case was dropped when the victim refused to give evidence. And it looks as if he may use another name sometimes too – that's what I'm still looking into."

"Interesting. Anything about his work life?"

"Yes. I found an old reference on LinkedIn for him. He described himself as a 'personal agent', whatever that means. Perhaps a bodyguard or something. All a bit mysterious, boss, and not entirely wholesome."

"You're right, Eamon. Sounds like a nasty piece of work. Look, can you get onto Derivest and tell them we urgently need to speak with their Mr Gilbert. Don't give any details, just say it's police business. And don't let them put you off – rattle them if needs be. If this dude gets back to the States, we'll never see him again, and I'm not having some cowboy slipping a Mickey Finn into the drink of one of my officers and getting away with it."

"Ah, don't worry, boss. We have the registration of his hired car from the hotel. If he's still in the Republic, we'll nab him."

"OK, Eamon. Best get on then."

When Flynn had left Lyons' office, her phone rang almost immediately.

"Good morning, Maureen. It's Liam O'Higgins here. Just thought I'd bring you up to date on our adventures out on the Newcastle Road."

"Hi, Liam. Thanks. What gives?"

"We have decided to go in tonight while chummy is inside. Even if he is just at the end of the chain, we'll get something from him in any case – my boys and girls have some interesting interrogation techniques that you don't want to know about. I was calling to see if you want any of yours to be in on it?"

"I'm not sure. I'll ask Sally Fahy if she wants to go. What time is it kicking off?"

"We're meeting at half past eight. I'm going to position cars on all of the roads out of there in case he gets past us somehow, and we'll have a team going into the house. Is Sally firearms trained?"

"Yes, she is, and she's damn good with a gun too. I've seen her in action. But surely you don't think this guy will be armed, do you?" Lyons said.

"He could be, and if he is and he shoots one of my guys we won't look too clever if we've left all our weapons at home. Anyway, it will frighten the you-know-what out of him when he sees a few sub-machine guns pointed at his sorry ass."

"Great. Sounds like fun. I'll have a word and let you know by lunchtime. OK?"

"Yes, fine. Cheers."

Chapter Nineteen

When Jed Gilbert left the hotel in Clifden, he drove back along the N59 towards Galway. At Recess, he pulled the car over onto the wide layby that was normally used for coaches visiting the souvenir shop and cafe that was popular with tourists in the summer months.

He took out his mobile phone and called Chuck Deri.

"Jesus, Jed, what time of the goddamn morning do you call this?"

"Sorry, boss. But we have a problem."

"What's that then?" Deri said.

"The Irish cops sent a girlie up to my hotel last night undercover to try and get me to talk. They know there's something iffy going on."

"Shit! What did you do?"

"I gave her a powder and took her home and had a good look around her place, but didn't find anything. I think they were just fishing."

"Is the girl OK? You didn't hurt her, did you?"

"Na, she'll be fine. She'll have a headache and feel goofy for a few days, but no lasting damage. And I was careful in her apartment too. They won't find a trace. It's a pity, she was a little cutie."

"Well, you'd better get away from there. And for fuck's sake keep us out of this. I don't pay you stupid amounts of money to bring shit home. Got it?"

"Yeah, sure, don't worry, Chuck, I'm not an idiot. You won't hear from me again for a few days. Then I'll see you in Logan."

"Before you go, did you get anywhere with the authorities over our licenses?"

"No, I didn't have a chance. But I think that'll be OK. They've been sweetened up a good bit already."

"I wish I had your confidence, Jed. This is important to us, you know that."

"Chill, Chuck. Have faith. It'll be fine."

* * *

By the time he got to the outskirts of Athlone, Gilbert needed a coffee and some breakfast. He had left the Alcock and Brown too early to avail of their hospitality, and his stomach was rumbling.

He took the exit off the M6 signposted for Athlone, and drove on down the dual carriageway towards the town. As he got close, there was a massive roundabout with seven roads leading off it, one of which was the entrance to a large petrol filling station that had a cafe and shop attached.

Gilbert drove onto the roundabout, or 'traffic circle' in his language, and immediately became confused about which way he should be travelling. He started down one of the exits on the wrong side of the road, and a second later a large, muddy, Mitsubishi 4x4 half-cab truck came out of the petrol station and smashed into the front of his car.

Gilbert was thrown against the steering wheel and hit his head on the A-pillar of the little rented Ford. By the time he started to come around and realise what had happened, an angry man in his fifties, dressed in working clothes, was at the driver's window of the rented car shouting abuse in through the glass at Jed.

Jed found the button to lower the window.

"Hey, take it easy, fella. It's just a fender bender."

But the driver of the truck wasn't going to be pacified that easily. He reached in through the opening and grabbed Gilbert by the shirt and started shouting, "Ye feckin eejit! Look what you've done to my jeep! I'll be off the road for days now, and it's all your fault – bloody Yank!"

But Jed was in luck, if you could call it that. Two uniformed Gardaí from the local station had been in the cafe having their morning coffee when they saw the whole episode through the enormous plate glass window.

"Here we go, Conor. Another bloody tourist that doesn't know which side of the road to drive on. Let's go and have a word," Kevin Roche said.

The Athlone Gardaí were well used to foreigners driving hire cars that found themselves in trouble, and they had to admit that the signage and layout just at that particular point was very confusing – even for the locals.

"Isn't that yer man that has the welding shop over in Baylough," Conor said to his colleague as they donned their uniform caps and started walking towards the melee.

"That's him, all right. Billy Lynch if I'm not mistaken. Ah, don't mind him. He's all hot air."

The two Gardaí calmed things down, although it was clear that neither vehicle was in a driveable state. Conor took several photographs with his mobile phone, while Lynch called back to his business and asked his number two to arrange a tow truck to get his jeep off the road. The two Gardaí helped Gilbert push his steaming Ford Focus to the side, leaving a pool of oil and broken glass and plastic on the tarmac.

"You'd better come into town with us, sir. We can call the rental company from the station and let them know what's happened. They'll probably arrange for a replacement car for you so you can continue your journey."

Gilbert was very uneasy at this suggestion.

"It's OK, officer, you can just leave me here. I need to get a coffee and something to eat anyway, and I can call the car hire company myself," he said, hoping that the police would be thankful that they didn't have to become further involved.

Conor, the more experienced of the two Gardaí, had walked away out of earshot of the little group and was on his radio. He had called in the registration number of Gilbert's car, and after a few minutes, got a rather surprising message. He walked back to where his colleague was still engaged with the two drivers.

"And who's going to pay for the damage to my car, and compensate me for being off the road? I'm fierce busy just now. This is all I need," Lynch said, giving the American sour looks.

"That'll be all taken care of, Mr Lynch. Have no fear. It looks quite cut and dried to me. And I have photographs too, so the car rental company will look after it."

"I should bloody hope so!" Lynch said.

Conor re-joined the little huddle.

"Mr Gilbert, I'm afraid I'm going to have to ask you to come into the station to make a statement about this accident. We don't want the insurers to try and wriggle out of paying for the damage to Mr Lynch's jeep, now, do we?"

"Is that really necessary, officer? I need to be on my way as quickly as I can, and I'm quite happy to admit that it was my fault. I have some important business matters to attend to in Dublin."

Conor reached to his belt and released the set of handcuffs that were fastened to it.

"If you'd just come along with us please, sir, and best not to make a fuss. Resisting arrest will only add to your troubles. Kevin, will you get Mr Gilbert's suitcase and other belongings from the Focus and put them in our car. Thanks."

Billy Lynch looked on, somewhat perplexed, but he decided not to say anything. He'd never seen anyone put in handcuffs before following a road traffic accident, but he supposed the Gardaí knew what they were doing, and he decided not to interfere.

* * *

It was almost lunchtime by the time Lyons got the call. The Athlone Gardaí had taken their time processing the fallout from the accident with Jed Gilbert. He had been charged with driving without due care and attention, and because he had no Irish driver's license, he had been informed that it would be necessary for him to attend court to receive his punishment.

"Not likely," he said to himself as the desk sergeant handed him the citation.

Athlone had then called Clifden and spoken to Seán Mulholland, and it was him who telephoned Lyons to give her the good news.

"Hello, Maureen. Look, Athlone have just been on to me. They have your man Gilbert there at the station. He drove his car up the wrong side of the road and into a jeep. Luckily, two of the lads were at the scene and had the good sense to call it in. What do you want them to do with him?"

"Fantastic, Seán. That's great news. Ask them to hang on to him for us. I'll send a car in to collect him. I want him here for questioning about Mary's big night out!"

"Oh, yes, I heard about that, poor lass. Is she OK, do you think?"

"She's fine. She's in good hands. Pascal will look after her. But I might get her to come in to help with Mr Gilbert's interview if she's up to it – what do you think?"

"God, Maureen, you're a fierce woman altogether. You'll have him grovelling at your feet before long," Mulholland said.

"That's the idea, Séan. Turns out he has a bit of previous too. I'm looking forward to this!"

* * *

Far from shrinking from the prospect of meeting Jed Gilbert again, Mary Fallon was delighted to receive the call from Lyons.

"Wow, that's great, Inspector. I'll just clear it with Pascal, and then I'll be in. How long will it take him to get from Athlone?" Fallon said.

"Don't worry about that. You'll be here before him – but in any case, we'll keep him for you!"

"Great! See you soon."

When Mary told Pascal Brosnan of her plan, he was a bit sceptical.

"Are you sure, girl? Have you not seen enough of the blaggard to do you?"

"Let's just say I have some unfinished business with Mr Gilbert. I'm not letting him get the better of me!"

"Fair enough. Off you go then. Let me know how you get on," Brosnan said, not totally convinced that Mary's plan was a good idea.

Chapter Twenty

Gilbert kept his powder dry when he was collected from Athlone Garda station. He would play his cards when he got in front of a senior officer in Galway, and get himself out of the pickle he had landed himself in. He'd done this before. He had no doubt that he would be able to talk his way out of more or less any situation involving the authorities.

When he arrived at Mill Street, he was booked in by the desk sergeant and shown to an interview room. He still said nothing, other than to confirm his name. The desk sergeant asked if he needed a drink or to use the bathroom, but Gilbert declined both.

Lyons and Fallon let themselves into the interview room where Gilbert was seated.

"Hello again," Mary Fallon said to the man. She was now dressed in her Garda uniform, and managed to look quite severe. Gilbert looked at her briefly, but said nothing.

"May I remind you that you are still under caution, Mr Gilbert, or whatever your real name is. This interview is being recorded." Lyons went on to recite the time, date and a list of those present in the room for the tape machine.

"Well, Mr Gilbert, perhaps you'd like to start by telling us about last night in the hotel in Clifden. It appears that you drugged one of my officers and then searched her dwelling. What were you looking for?" Lyons said.

"That's nonsense. I did nothing of the kind. And may I remind you that I am an American citizen, and I have rights under international law."

Lyons took out Gilbert's passport from her folder. It had been removed from his suitcase in Athlone Garda station. She opened it deliberately in front of him.

"It doesn't look to me like a diplomatic passport, Mr Gilbert. You may well be an American citizen, but you still have to obey the laws of Ireland, and in this country, drugging a serving member of the Gardaí, or anyone for that matter, is a serious offence."

"I don't know what you're talking about. Now why don't you just let me out of here. I have places to go, people to see."

Just then, there was a knock at the door. John O'Connor stepped into the room and gestured for Lyons to step out for a moment.

Lyons paused the interview, got up and left.

Outside, O'Connor handed her another folder.

"Sinéad got back with the urine analysis, boss. Rohypnol. Not a massive dose, but enough to put poor Mary out for the count. And I got some more information on your man from Inspector Flynn. He used to be called Jerome Gibson, and he has quite a rap sheet – some of it quite unpleasant. We also got some suspicious-looking capsules in his wash bag. I've asked Sinéad to see if they match what he slipped into Mary's drink."

"Great. Thanks, John. Good work. Let me know about the medication as soon as it comes through."

While Lyons was out of the room, and the recorder was switched off temporarily, Mary Fallon spoke to Gilbert.

"So, what did you slip into my drink?"

"I don't know what you mean. You had too many vodkas, and I had to help you home," he lied.

"That's funny. I was drinking water with lime cordial – not vodka. So, I don't think so."

"You mean I was paying for liquor and you were drinking water?"

"Exactly. But if you ever get out of here you can apply to the hotel for a refund. I'm not a complete fool!" Mary said.

Gilbert just shrugged and after a few more minutes of tense silence, Lyons re-entered and recommenced the formal interview.

"Right, Mr Gilbert, or should we call you Jerome Gibson?"

Gilbert flinched a little at the sound of his other name, but recovered quickly.

"Look, Inspector, I've already said, you have no right to detain me here. I want consular assistance from the United States embassy and an attorney. I'm saying nothing more."

"Very well, but you should know that we now have evidence that you are in possession of a class C amphetamine which is illegal in this country, and we will be charging you later with that, and other offences. We will also be in contact with the police in the USA to inform them and see what other information they may like to share with us. If I were you, I'd be looking forward to quite a long stay in Ireland."

When Lyons and Fallon got back to the main office, Lyons arranged for a duty solicitor to be retained to represent Jed Gilbert.

"OK, Mary? I'll be charging him with assault on a Garda later, as well as a few other things we can easily pin on him. He'll get done for possession for sure, and I'll have a word upstairs and see what else we might be able to charge him with. Do you want to hang around?"

"Yes, boss. I'd like to wait to see him charged, if that's OK."

"Of course. While you're waiting, can you give John a hand with Gilbert's stuff. Let's see what his mobile phone has to say for itself. And see if there's any paperwork in his bag that could be useful to us as well."

* * *

Detective Superintendent Mick Hays was in his office when he received a call from Chief Superintendent Finbarr Plunkett's personal assistant. He was wanted in the senior man's office.

"Come in, Mick. Have a seat. How's everything?" Plunkett said.

Hays was a little wary. He had had many conversations that started this way with his boss, but ended badly for him.

"All good, thanks, sir. How can I help?"

"Straight to the point, eh? OK. Well, I hear you have a Yank downstairs – something to do with a little car accident over in Athlone. Is that right?"

"Yes, sir. But there's a bit more to it than that."

Hays went on to fill Plunkett in on what he had been told by Maureen Lyons about Gilbert's antics the previous night. Plunkett shuffled uneasily in his seat.

"Hmm. How do you think it will go, Mick?"

"Well, he's going to be charged with a number of offences, and given that he's obviously a flight risk, we'll be looking to remand him. Why? Have you had a phone call?"

"Nothing official yet, but I'm expecting it. Gilbert is involved with the mining company that are looking to start some exploration out near Clifden. It's very sensitive, and of course, there are politicians involved."

"Yeah, but we can't have some guy going around drugging our officers and getting up to God knows what.

And don't forget, we have a murder investigation in train that may be somehow connected as well."

"Is the Yank a suspect?" Plunkett said.

"Not yet. There's no evidence to connect him directly to the death of Davin Faherty. But we haven't really started digging into it yet. He may be involved. We'll know soon."

"OK. Well, look, Mick, for God sake go carefully. I'd say we have about twenty-four hours before things start to get all political on us, and then well, you never know what might happen. Are you sure he has no diplomatic connections?"

"None that we can find, and he hasn't played that particular card – not convincingly anyway. Just mouthing off about being an American citizen and all that guff."

"Right. Well, look. Stay at it till you hear from me, and let me know if you get anything further on this guy. But I'd say we need to be ready for a bit of an onslaught. I've seen this before and it can easily go badly against us. OK?"

"Yes, of course, sir."

Plunkett looked down at his desk and started shuffling pieces of paper – the well-practiced signal that the meeting was over. Hays got up and went back to his office where he called Lyons.

"Hi. It's me. Have you got a minute?" he said to her.

"Sure. Do you want me to pop up?"

"Could you? I've just been in with Finbarr."

"Oh-oh. OK. I'm on my way."

* * *

"So, what did the chief want?" Lyons said when she was seated opposite her partner nursing a cup of fresh coffee.

Hays went on to relay the substance of the meeting with his senior officer.

"Do you think he's linked to the murder of Davin Faherty?" Hays said.

"I wouldn't put it past him. He has a record as long as your arm in a different name – mostly assaults, GBH, that sort of thing. He's done time in the States too. But we've nothing to connect him – not yet anyway."

"Well, that's something. At least the politicians won't be baying for blood to save a felon – at least I hope not. How's that enquiry going?"

"It's not. Not really. All we know is that Faherty was poisoned with arsenic and then dumped in the bog. Forensics are working hard to try and get more from the scene. But the trail will be going cold now, so I'm not very optimistic. Oh, and we found Davin Faherty's car in the barn at his place all covered up nice and snugly in a tarpaulin."

"I see. What did the brother say about that?"

"We haven't questioned him about it yet. I've been keeping that up our sleeve, but maybe it's time to have a word."

"Well, you know best. Do you need anything from me?"

"What I need is some evidence, Mick."

Chapter Twenty-one

Liam O'Higgins gathered his team together for a briefing before driving out to the Newcastle Road. Sally Fahy had drawn a gun from the armoury using a permit signed off by Hays, and had checked the weapon over carefully before placing it snugly in a holster attached to her belt and covering it from view with her jacket. The entire team were wearing bulletproof vests, and they looked quite intimidating as they gathered round to hear their orders for the night.

"Right, listen up everyone," O'Higgins said, pointing to an enlarged map of the locale pinned to an easel in the corner of the room.

"As soon as our friend arrives, we'll put two vehicles across the road, here and here, blocking any escape. Four of you will go into the house – two at the front and two at the back. We'd better tell the guy in the take-away what's happening, but not till the last minute. Sally, would you like to be one of the team to go in?"

"Yes, sir, if that's OK?"

"Of course. Just keep your wits about you – we don't know what we're up against here. Now, has everybody got a working radio?"

A murmur of assent went around the team.

"Right, well don't forget to use them. We need to stay in touch at all times. And when we get in there, don't mess about. Disable chummy as quickly as possible. Look for anyone else that might be hiding out in there too – you just never know. When the place is clear, we'll get the lads to get in and clear the place of the plants and equipment. Any questions?"

No one asked any, so they prepared to go to their vehicles.

* * *

The first mistake that the man who was tending to the grow house made was to turn up at more or less the same time every night. It showed him up as a bit of an amateur, which probably meant that he was just a sort of gardener – hardly the brains behind the whole operation.

At just after half past nine in the evening, he came strolling down the road dressed in his usual outfit, with a hoodie hiding his features from view. He did his usual reconnaissance walk past the place and then back before slipping down the side path and in through the back door.

O'Higgins, who was positioned in the observation house directing operations, instructed the cars to move into position at each end of the road, and told the officers in them not to let anyone through in either direction until the operation was stood down.

After another few minutes, he issued the instruction to go into the house to the two teams standing by.

Sally Fahy was asked to go in the back way after the lead officer had kicked in the door – an easy task, as the wood was partly rotten in any case. The front door needed a little more persuasion, so the 'big red key' was deployed, and within twenty seconds, the house was swarming with Gardaí shouting and pointing their weapons in a menacing fashion.

It didn't take them long to locate the man who had been adjusting the lights which were poised over what looked like a sea of green plants, stretching for several metres along the full length of a makeshift bench. Caught cold, he turned towards the two nearest Gardaí and put his hands up.

"Jesus! OK, OK, I give up. Don't shoot."

One of the uniformed officers moved in and patted the man down. He removed the hood from his head, and as soon as he did so, Sally Fahy piped up, "Hello, Laughlin. Fancy seeing you here!"

The other Gardaí looked at her, somewhat puzzled. One of them said, "Do you know this bloke, Sally?"

"I certainly do. Meet Laughlin Faherty, folks – small-time farmer from Boolagare. You'll probably find his old Land Rover parked somewhere nearby," she said, smirking a little. She wasn't expecting to see Laughlin at all.

"OK. Cuff him, caution him and bring him in. I'm sure Inspector O'Higgins would like a word."

As Laughlin Faherty was shoved into the back of one of the marked squad cars that had driven up to the front of the little cottage, a team from forensics appeared to examine the site carefully and collect evidence. Faherty's fingerprints would be recorded to ensure that he couldn't worm his way out of his involvement with the operation in some way, and the team hoped to find traces of others that were known to them in the place too.

Inspector O'Higgins decided not to interview Faherty that evening. He felt that a night in the cells might soften the young man up a bit, so he arranged to come in at nine o'clock the following morning. But before they all went their separate ways, O'Higgins spoke to Sally Fahy.

"Thanks for your help, Sally. It was great that you were able to identify Faherty. That'll save us some time and effort. Be sure to put Inspector Lyons in the picture, won't you?"

"Yes, of course. And thanks for letting me tag along. I wouldn't have missed it for the world."

* * *

Fahy went back to Mill Street to check in her gun. She didn't like having it on her, and as it hadn't been used, it was just a simple matter of getting the desk sergeant to count the live rounds and log it back into the armoury.

When she had done that, she felt that she still smelled of cannabis, so she went to the washroom and scrubbed her face and hands, which helped, but didn't eliminate the scent totally.

Then she called Maureen Lyons who was at home in Salthill.

"Hi, Inspector, it's Sally here. I just thought you'd like to know that we've finished up at the grow house out on the Newcastle Road. But you'll never guess what."

"You're right, Sally, I'll never guess."

"The guy that was tending to the place was only Laughlin Faherty. Caught him red-handed. He's here in custody now. O'Higgins is going to tackle him in the morning."

"Hmm... I wonder," Lyons said.

"What, boss?"

"I wonder if I shouldn't come in and have a little chat with Mr Faherty right now. He could be feeling quite vulnerable just at the moment. It's a good time to get them to talk."

"Oh, right. Would you like me to stay here and lend a hand?" Fahy volunteered.

"OK, that would be great. Do you mind?"

"No, of course not. I'm too wound up to sleep for a good while anyway, and I'd like to hear what he has to say for himself."

"OK. I'll be in in about twenty minutes. Who is the night man tonight on the desk?"

"That's Danny Reilly, boss."

"OK. Have a word with him, will you, and square him off. And find out who the duty solicitor is as well, will you, just in case Faherty wants to be represented?" Lyons said.

* * *

Half an hour later Lyons and Fahy entered the interview room where Laughlin Faherty had been taken. He had declined the services of a lawyer, but had been reminded that if he changed his mind at any point, all he had to do was say so, and a solicitor would be provided for him.

Lyons made the necessary introductions and went through the usual ritual for the tape, recording the date, time, those present and so on.

"I need to remind you that you are still under caution, Laughlin, so anything you say here is admissible as evidence. Now, I don't want to be here all night, so what's been going on?"

Faherty just shrugged and said nothing. He looked sullen and dejected, and was quite obviously very uncomfortable.

"OK, then, tell us how you got involved with growing cannabis plants," Lyons said.

Faherty looked back at Lyons and said, "No comment."

"I see. Well, that's fine, Laughlin. You just keep saying that and we'll let nature take its course. You'll be here for a good while, and we'll get you remanded until your trial, so you'd better start thinking about who is going to tend to your animals and the farm out at Boolagare."

Lyons started getting her papers together.

"C'mon, Sally. I need a drink."

The two Gardaí got up and made for the door.

"Wait! I'll tell you what you want if you let me out of here," Faherty said.

Lyons looked at Fahy and nodded slightly, and the two of them went back to the table and sat down.

"Go on then," Lyons prompted, having restarted the tape recorder.

"The drugs were Davin's gig – not mine. He was looking after that place, and when he died, they approached me to take it over. So, I agreed. I needed the extra money."

"I see. And who exactly is 'they', Laughlin?" Lyons said.

"Ah, Jesus, I can't tell you that. I'm no grass. They'd fucking kill me!"

"OK. Well, here is how it's going to go. Tomorrow morning Inspector Liam O'Higgins will be here and he'll be expecting you to tell him a lot more than you've told us. Then you'll be taken before a judge and most likely be remanded – so think hard overnight about what that means for you."

Lyons nodded at Fahy again, and they terminated the interview and left the room.

Chapter Twenty-two

Liam O'Higgins arrived at Mill Street bright and early the following morning. He had Laughlin Faherty moved from his cell to an interview room, and wasted no time in settling down with the man. Faherty had declined the offer of a solicitor, so O'Higgins got straight down to the serious matter of questioning the suspect to try and find out about the gang that were operating it.

Faherty staunchly refused to give up any names. He claimed that he knew his taskmaster only by the name of Maurice, and he was fairly certain that this was not the man's real name.

"Have you met this Maurice character?" O'Higgins asked.

"No. It was all done over the phone. But there was very little communication at all. He just wanted me to go to the little house every evening – check the temperature, the lamps, CO_2 levels and humidity. Feed the plants – that's all."

"So, you never met this Maurice then?"

"No."

"How did you get paid?"

"Money was left at the house every Friday for me."

"How much?"

Faherty didn't reply at once, so O'Higgins prompted him again.

"Two hundred a week. Not much really when you think what all that stuff was worth."

"Were you involved in the harvesting of the weed?"

"No. Davin might have been. But the crop was a couple of weeks off being ready, I think."

"Was that the full extent of your involvement in this business, Laughlin? It would be better if you'd come clean now with us. If we find out later that you've been lying, it will make matters a good deal worse for you."

"No, that's it. There's no more to tell. To be honest, I wasn't happy about it at all, but it seemed like handy money, and I don't exactly make a fortune from scratching around out on the bog now, do I?"

"What about the mining?" O'Higgins said.

"What mining?"

"The mining that Derivest are planning for that whole area out where you have your farm. Surely that will make you some good, honest money?"

Laughlin Faherty sat back in the chair and laughed – a genuine, hearty laugh.

"You don't actually believe that shite, do ye?"

"What do you mean? Aren't the Americans filing for a license to explore for copper and maybe gold out there?"

"Jesus! There's one born every minute. Surely you don't believe all that nonsense, do you?"

"What do you mean, Laughlin?"

"If I tell you what's really going on, can I get out of here with no charges?"

"That's not up to me. But if you have information that could be useful to us, it might help your position. But you'll have to wait till I get Inspector Lyons down here. Don't go away, I'll be back."

O'Higgins paused the interview and went to find Maureen Lyons.

She was in her office on the first floor, and O'Higgins knocked before being invited in.

"Come in, Liam. What gives?"

"Well, your man downstairs says he has information on the mining operation out near Clifden. He seems to think there's some kind of scam being worked. I thought you might like to hear what he has to say."

"Yes, I would. But do you not think he's just bluffing to improve his own position?"

"No, actually, I don't. Oddly, I think Laughlin Faherty is quite an honest man. I've interviewed quite a number of people who have been involved in drugs, and he's not typical. Not at all."

"OK. Let's go and see what he has to say. We still have Jed Gilbert in custody in any case if there is something iffy going on."

* * *

"Right, Laughlin, you have the stage – now tell us what you know," O'Higgins said when he and Lyons had re-joined the interview.

"What do I get out of it?"

O'Higgins was first to speak.

"Growing cannabis plants is treated as a class C offence and is subject to a minimum term of twelve months in jail, but can be extended for up to fourteen years, depending on the scale and degree of the person's involvement."

"That's no good to me, pal. I told you, I need to get out of here. Who's going to look after my sheep?"

O'Higgins looked at Lyons, who nodded imperceptibly.

"Well, depending on what you have to tell us, we might be able to argue that you were just stopping by to get some weed for your own personal use. That just carries a caution, so you'd be out later today. But only if you have some really good information for us."

"OK. I'll start at the beginning then. About a year ago, this American bloke rocks up to our place saying he wants to have a chat. Davin and I were both there at the time, so we brings him in and sits him down in the kitchen. After a whole load of bullshit about his ancestors coming from Ballyhaunis, he gets to the point. He represents a mining company, and they want to do some soil tests on our land. He said there might be minerals there and if that was the case, we could both do very well out of it."

"Did he offer you any money to let them do the sampling?"

"No, course not. It was all 'jam tomorrow'."

"What did you say?"

"Davin was dead against it. He didn't want the land interfered with, and he didn't want to hear anything about mining on it either. He was odd like that. A bit of a traditionalist for all his whacky ways. But I was all for it. The chance to make some money from the old place at last, so I persuaded Davin to let the sample bores go ahead."

"Then what happened?"

"About six weeks later this guy's team of geologists came along and drilled a few holes into the bog. Apparently, they were doing this all over the place. The holes were very small and didn't affect anyone at all. They took core samples and went away with them."

"OK. So, when did you hear from the American next?" Lyons asked, keen to get on with the story.

"It must have been about two months. He came back in person and said that the core samples had been positive, and he was getting his legal boys to draw up papers and submit an application for the mining. But it was all bullshit."

"How do you mean?"

"Well, after he had gone, I went back around where the holes had been drilled and extracted my own samples. I took them into the University here in Galway, and had them analysed. Nothing. Not a whiff of any metal ores. A bit of arsenic, but no copper or gold or anything else other than limestone and turf!"

"So, what was his game?" O'Higgins said.

"Here's the clever bit. I reckon he was playing both sides against each other. He concocted some bogus analysis to keep his parent company interested and put it about around here that there was a good chance that there was copper, if not gold, under the bog. What do you think that did to land prices?"

O'Higgins looked at Lyons.

"It would have put them up – a lot. But how would that benefit Mr Gilbert?"

"That's for you lot to find out. You're the detectives after all – but I reckon if you look hard enough, you'll find that Mr Gilbert is the beneficial owner of quite a lot of what we think of as common land out near my place."

"Did you tell him what you had discovered?"

"Not likely. I was keeping that for another day. Information is power, Inspector."

"Have you any paperwork that backs up what you've told us?" Lyons said.

"Course I have. I keep it well secured out at the farm. I have the report from Galway University and a few other bits and bobs about land sales recently. So, do I get out of here now?"

"Not so fast, Laughlin. This could all be a story. We need a few minutes to chat amongst ourselves. We'll be back in a while."

* * *

Outside in the corridor, Lyons and O'Higgins had a chat.

"What do you reckon, Maureen? Is it feasible?"

"Yes, but that doesn't make it true. Maybe I need to go and have another little chat with our Mr Gilbert. We can't keep him much longer without getting him before a judge, but I reckon he'll get remanded anyway."

"OK. What about Faherty?"

"He'll keep."

Before Lyons spoke to Jed Gilbert again, she decided to consult Mick Hays. He was in his office, so she went up and into where he was working on some report or other for Division.

"Hi, you," he said when he saw her. The interruption was welcome.

"Hi. Sorry to barge in. Have you got a minute?"

"Of course. What's up?"

Lyons related what Laughlin Faherty had told her about Jed Gilbert and his plans, and Hays listened intently.

"OK, Maureen, this changes things a bit. Look I'd better get onto the US embassy and see if they want to get involved. Chances are they won't, but they like to be asked in these situations. I'd better brief Plunkett as well in case he gets an earful from Merrion Square. How do you want to play it?"

"I'm going to see what paperwork Faherty has to back up his story. I need someone to start digging on land transactions out west as well – see if there have been any sales recently and what else has been going on. Surely you can't sell common land – or buy it for that matter?"

"I'm not familiar with the laws around that, but I could give our old friend James McMahon a call and see if he knows anything. Would that help?" Hays said.

"Yes, it would. I have to admit to being quite out of my depth on this one, Mick. And another thing, can you keep Plunkett off my back for a while till we see what's what. I don't need him barging in and crashing around all over this till we get a good bit further on with it."

"I'll do my best, love," Hays said, "but you did want to get into serious crime after all. Be careful what you wish for."

"Not helpful, Superintendent, not helpful at all," she said, getting up to leave wondering exactly how best to proceed.

* * *

"Sally, can you go and collect Laughlin Faherty from downstairs for me. I want to take him out home to Boolagare and see what paperwork he has to back up his accusations about Gilbert. Then we'll see if we can let him off with a caution, or if we need to press charges."

"OK, boss, but what about Gilbert?"

"Get Eamon to take him around to the court before Judge Meehan finishes up and have him charged with ABH. Make sure he's remanded – you know, flight risk, all that sort of stuff. And keep an eye out for a call from Mick too. He's contacting the US embassy to see if they have any interest in the man."

"OK. Give me ten minutes and I'll see you downstairs with Faherty."

Chapter Twenty-three

On the way out to Faherty's farm there was very little conversation in Lyons' car. Sally Fahy was seated in the back beside Laughlin, and she did try to gently probe him a bit more about his relationship with his brother, but didn't get very far.

"Tell me, Laughlin, how exactly did you get along with Davin?"

"Hmph... not well, not well at all. We disagreed about almost everything."

"But you must have known what he was up to with the drugs. Did that not bother you?"

"I didn't. He never said anything, except that he used to disappear a lot and sometimes wouldn't be back for days on end – sometimes even weeks."

"Were you not curious about where he got the money to buy that nice VW Golf from?"

"Look, Sergeant, we had nothing at all in common. He was lazy and always after the quick buck. I believe in earning my money through hard work, so I let him get on with it."

"Did you ever have real disagreements – like proper fights – violent, that sort of thing?"

"No, not that. I wouldn't waste my energy on him."

And then the car fell silent again as they passed Maam Cross and Recess.

When they got to the Fahertys' place, Lyons pulled the car into the yard and stopped.

"OK, Laughlin, I want you to show me the paperwork that supports your theory about Gilbert and the soil samples."

"Fair enough. Have you got a torch? It's in the barn."

Lyons used the light on her phone to penetrate the darkness inside the musty barn. Faherty went to the side where there was a workbench. Underneath the bench he pulled out an old metal trunk and opened it to reveal sheafs of paper all neatly gathered in elastic bands. Lyons could see that some of the pages had the emblem of NUI Galway on them. Faherty handed the papers to her.

Lyons took the files outside to examine them in better light. While she was gone, Fahy asked Laughlin about Davin's car.

"How come Davin's VW is here in the barn, Laughlin?"

"I dunno. He must have been going drinking with his mates or something and got the bus, or a lift. He didn't say anything to me."

"Did he often do that – leave his car here when he went out?" Fahy asked.

"Sometimes."

"And you've no idea who would want to do him harm, Laughlin? He was murdered after all."

"I dunno. I told you, we didn't mix in the same circles. God knows what he was into. He must have been mixed up with some right rogues what with the drugs and all."

"Did he ever mention that he was being threatened, or owed anyone a lot of money?"

"No, he didn't. And he always seemed to have lots of cash – not that he ever paid any of the bills here, like the electric or anything."

Lyons came back into the barn.

"Looks like you may have been right, Laughlin. Of course, this isn't conclusive, but it does support your theory that there are no metals worth bothering about here in the bog. We will have to have these documents authenticated at the University, but that's just a formality."

"So, what happens now?" Faherty asked.

"You'll have to come into Clifden with us to be formally cautioned. Then I'm going to ask you to report to the Garda Station there twice a week till we get all this sorted out. I'll tell Sergeant Mulholland to expect you. Have you got a passport?"

"No, I don't. Why, are you afraid I'll run away?"

"Which days suit you to report in?"

"Any days – makes no difference to me. Let's say Tuesdays and Fridays. OK?"

"Fine, Sally, can you set that up for me?"

"Yes, sure, boss."

Laughlin Faherty was taken into Clifden where Lyons, who was authorised by virtue of her rank to issue a formal adult caution, went through the procedure with him. Mulholland was advised of the arrangements, and he said he would get someone to drop Faherty back out to his farm.

"No, I have to collect the Land Rover from the city. I'll take a lift back with these two, if that's OK?"

So, Lyons and Fahy drove Faherty back to the city and dropped him off at Mill Street Garda Station.

* * *

When Mick Hays called James McMahon, the architect was surprised to hear from him quite so soon.

"Hello, Mick. Two calls in almost as many days – I'm honoured. What can I do for you today?"

"Hi, James. I'm not sure if you've heard anything, but there's a spot of bother over that mineral exploration thing that's been going on out west. I can't go into the details, but it looks like there's been some hanky-panky afoot. Have you heard anything?"

"No, it's not really our thing to be honest. But I'm well got with some of the councillors out in Clifden. I could make a call if you like?"

Hays filled McMahon in with as much detail as he dared, and asked him to see what he could find out without alerting anyone to the reason for his enquiries.

"Ah, don't worry, Mick. They are used to me nosing around. I'll see what I can dig up for you. And did you think any more about buying a place here in the city?"

"God, James, we haven't really had time. Why, is there something we should be looking at?"

"There's a small block of apartments just being finished off down near the docks. I hear the builder is in a spot of bother and needs to shift a couple of them pronto. I'm sure he'd offer a good deal for cash. If you like, I could give him a call for you?"

"I'll have a chat with Maureen later and let you know. But can I ask, James, what's in it for you?" Hays said.

"God, Mick, always the policeman, eh. If I can get yer man a quick deal and keep him out of trouble then where else will he go next time he's going to build something?"

"Oh, right. Yeah – tell you what, give him a call and set up a meet. I'll persuade Maureen to make some time. And, James, thanks."

* * *

When Lyons had finished with Laughlin Faherty and was back in the station, she went in search of Hays. Again, she found him in his office.

"Ah, the very girl I was looking for. What can I do for you?" he said.

"You first – what do you want me for?"

Hays went on to outline the discussion he had had with James McMahon about their property aspirations.

"God, Mick. I haven't really got any time to devote to that just now. This Gilbert thing is ramping up, that's what I came to see you about."

"OK. Well, would you be happy for me to look after the property thing and spend your money? This opportunity won't last long – then we can talk about Mr Gilbert."

"Would you? That would be great, and of course I trust you totally – no question. Just don't buy a boat!"

Hays smiled. He knew his partner wasn't a good seafarer, even though he enjoyed being on the water very much.

"Ha, ha, as if. Now, I've been talking to the US embassy in Dublin. It took a while but I got through to a senior consul eventually. They have no interest whatever in Mr Jed Gilbert, in fact I got the impression that if we decided to incarcerate him for a few years, it would be quite a relief."

"Nice one! So, we don't need to worry about them, at least. I'm fairly certain that the thing about the minerals will check out with NUI Galway as well. We'll just have to figure out exactly what to charge him with. I wish I knew if he was involved with Davin Faherty's death – that would be the clincher."

"Let's see what James comes back with. I mean, what do you think his motive for bumping off the lad might be?"

"That's what I can't figure out. But by all accounts, Davin was into all sorts. He might have found out what Gilbert was up to and tried to blackmail him or something."

"OK. Well, I presume Eamon will have got him remanded by now. Why don't we leave him till tomorrow and then both of us have a go at him – see if we can get him to talk?"

"Sounds like a plan. What time are you finished here?"

"About six, I reckon. You?"

"Same. Shall we go and get something to eat in O'Connaire's?"

"Yeah, good idea. I'll give Agnes a call and make a booking."

Chapter Twenty-four

Judge Meehan took his seat at the bench. He was looking uncharacteristically sour today.

"He's probably dropped a stroke on his golf handicap," Flynn said to himself.

The clerk of the court handed Meehan a sheet of paper which he studied for a moment.

"Well, Inspector, I haven't got all day," he said looking down at Flynn over his glasses.

Flynn stood and read the charges that they had decided to file against Jed Gilbert.

"Is the defendant represented in court?"

The duty solicitor who had been sitting at the front of the court with his legs folded, unwound his limbs and stood up.

"Yes, Judge."

"Very well then – what have you got to say for yourself?"

"My client," he said, half turning to Gilbert who was standing sullenly in the dock with a uniformed Garda on each side of him, "strenuously denies the charges, and furthermore, would like to protest in strong terms at the treatment he has received at the hands of the Gardaí."

"I understand your client is an American, is that right, Mr ehh…?"

The judge knew full well that the man who would attempt to get Jed Gilbert away from the grasp of the Gardaí was called O'Saughnessy, but he was feeling mischievous as well as grumpy today.

"O'Saughnessy, Judge, Anselm O'Saughnessy, and that is correct. He is expecting representation from the government of the USA to bring this sorry matter to a speedy conclusion at any minute."

Meehan looked across at Flynn as if expecting him to say something.

Flynn was back on his feet.

"We have been in contact with the American embassy in Dublin, Judge, just as a courtesy, you understand. So, they know the position."

"Are there any procedures that I should be aware of in train, Inspector?"

"No, Judge, none at all. To be honest, they seemed quite disinterested."

Meehan turned his attention back to the duty solicitor.

"In any case, Mr O'Saughnessy, this is Galway not the Wild West, and as long as I'm in charge here, what I say goes. Your client can argue the toss with President Trump later. Understood?"

O'Saughnessy nodded, but said nothing.

Meehan turned again to Eamon Flynn.

"Inspector, have you sufficient evidence to proceed?"

"Not as yet, Judge, but we are preparing a book of evidence, and we will be proceeding with the charges. It's also likely that further charges will be brought against Mr Gilbert in due course."

"Very well. Mr O'Saughnessy, I'm sure you will want to ask for bail on behalf of your client?"

"Eh, yes, of course, thank you, Judge. My client denies the allegations being made against him. He is of good character, and has no intention of going anywhere until this matter is cleared up. My client represents an American corporation with extensive interests in the area, and the prospect of creating several jobs and other opportunities for the local community."

Flynn was on his feet again.

"Judge, I'm afraid Mr O'Saughnessy is misinformed. His client has previous convictions in the United States for assault and other crimes, and has actually served jail time, albeit under another name. We have serious concerns that he may well try to flee the jurisdiction were he to be granted bail, so we would ask you to remand him until a full hearing can be arranged."

Meehan seemed to warm to the idea.

"Remanded to Castlerea to appear in two weeks' time again before me in person." He banged his gavel and started tidying away his papers.

O'Saughnessy was on his feet, but the clerk instructed him to sit down, telling him that the matter was concluded.

Gilbert erupted.

"You can't do this to me! I'm an American citizen. I have rights. You haven't heard the end of this," he shouted from the dock.

Meehan wasn't having it.

"Mr O'Saughnessy, I would advise you to get your client to calm down or I shall hold him in contempt. Guards, take him away, for God's sake."

Gilbert was led away by the two burly Gardaí. He was muttering protests, but none of it made any difference. He was taken to a waiting van with a cage in the back, and whisked off to the remand centre in Harristown, County Roscommon, an hour and a half's drive north of Galway.

* * *

Lyons was in her office when Flynn returned from the court.

"How did that go?" she said.

"As expected, he's been remanded to Castlerea. He was shouting the odds a bit about being American and all, but Meehan was having none of it. The judge was in flying form."

"Excellent, well done. It's a bit of a bugger having to drive all that way to question him again, but it's better than having him out on bail. Now, Eamon, time to have some fun."

"How's that, boss?"

"Let's give Gilbert's boss a call in Logan, Utah and cheer him up a bit."

"You're bad, Inspector, very bad!"

"I know. But don't you love it?" she said smiling and reaching for the telephone.

After a few minutes on hold, listening to country and western music, the phone was answered by a man with a gravelly voice and an American accent.

"Good morning, is that Mr Chuck Deri?" Lyons said. She had put the telephone on speaker so that Flynn could enjoy the dialogue.

"Yeah, this is Chuck – who's this?"

"My name is Senior Inspector Lyons from the police in Galway, Ireland. Can you confirm that a Mr Jed Gilbert is an employee of your company?"

"Jed, yeah, he sure is. Is he OK?"

"I'm sorry to have to inform you, but Mr Gilbert is in custody here. He's been charged with an assault on one of my officers and is being held on remand."

"You're kidding, right?"

"No, sir, I'm definitely not kidding. May I ask you in what capacity Mr Gilbert is employed?

"Shit! Oh, OK, yeah, he's a kind of Mr Fixit. He's been doing some work over in Ireland for us."

"And what exactly has he been fixing for you, Mr Deri?"

"We're looking into doing some mining for copper and other metals over there. Jed has been arranging the core samples and attending to some of the licensing issues. It's looking promising too. We're hoping to get going there next year."

"Mr Deri, may I ask where you have had the core samples analysed and what exactly they indicated?"

"Well now, that's kinda commercially sensitive, Inspector. I'm not sure I can give you that kind of information."

"As you wish, Mr Deri. Can you at least give me the name of the laboratory that did the analysis for your company?"

"I don't have that information at my fingertips, and anyway, Jed made all the arrangements, so why don't you ask him?"

"Very well. But you should know that there has been independent analysis carried out here on some of the core samples that allegedly gave positive indications for minerals, and the independent analysis contradicts what Mr Gilbert said that he found."

"What are you talking about, officer? That's bullshit!"

"Really. Well, that's not my problem, Mr Deri, but it could be yours. If I were you, I'd be checking this whole thing out very carefully before you spend millions of dollars digging up the bog."

"Look, officer, Mr Gilbert is a trusted employee of this company, and I'm sure whatever charges you have brought against him are just some kind of horrible mistake. Now, when can we get him back here to sort out the other business?"

"Hard to tell but it could be a couple of years if he gets jail time."

"You're kidding me! How the hell am I supposed to run a business under these conditions?"

"And by the way, you might like to look into Mr Gilbert's background too."

"What are you talking about? What do you know?"

"I'm afraid I couldn't possibly disclose that information, Mr Deri. It's too sensitive."

Eamon Flynn was sniggering at this, but managed to keep it quiet so as not to alert the American.

"Well, that's us about done here, Mr Deri. We just thought you needed to know what has been going on. I should tell you we may have further charges to bring against Mr Gilbert too – but we will keep you posted as things develop. You have a nice day now," Lyons said and finished the call.

The two Gardaí burst out laughing.

Chapter Twenty-five

Laughlin Faherty walked from Mill Street Garda station out as far as the old cottage where the cannabis had been cultivated, and then on a little bit further to collect his Land Rover. As he drove back out to Boolagare, he tried to process what had happened. How had he got mixed up in this business in the first place? It was stupid. He wasn't even going to make a great deal of money from the caper. By the time he'd put diesel into the jeep and driven in and back every evening, he hardly made anything. And there was the chance of being caught – which of course had now come to pass – and the associated problems. From now on he'd stick to scratching out a living in the fields that his father had clawed back from the wasteland, and avoid any further truck with drugs or those that supply them.

It was early evening by the time he got back home and got settled. He walked up across his few fields and checked on the animals. All seemed to be in order. The clouds were building out over the ocean, and he knew that there would be heavy rain in a few hours – he could smell it on the wind.

"Soon be time to bring the cattle to the factory," he said to himself, seeing that there was very little grazing left on the heathland. He strolled back to the house and went inside. He lit the fire that he had previously set in the large open hearth. He used dry kindling from under the hedgerows to start it, and then piled turf sods on in a pyramid shape till they caught and started to emit the highly scented blue smoke and orange flames.

He wasn't particularly hungry, but he knew he needed to eat something. There wasn't much food in the house. He went to the bread bin – the last resort – and found half a loaf of unsliced white bread that was a bit dry, but hadn't yet grown any mould. He took the breadknife from the drawer and cut two thick slices, then spread a generous coating of butter on each, followed by a layer of strawberry jam. He put the old aluminium kettle on to boil on the gas stove too, and it wasn't long before it was singing, ready for him to make a large mug of tea.

When he had eaten the meagre meal, he took out his diary and wrote it up. It had been a crazy few days, and it seemed the Gardaí still had no idea who had killed his brother. He thought some more about the approach they had had from the mining company, and wondered if it would come to anything. If only Davin had been a bit more in favour of it. If his brother had taken his advice, they could have sold up and put a good few euro in the bank. It would not have been a fortune, but it would have enabled Laughlin to buy a place closer to town and get away from this backbreaking work that he had inherited along with the rights to the land. Still, it didn't matter now.

He put more turf on the fire to ward off the evening chill. He was sitting in front of the hearth, listening to the flames flickering and the occasional crackle given off by the fuel when he heard a noise outside. Suddenly alert, he listened carefully for a moment, and there it was again. Could there be someone out there? He hardly thought so. They got very few callers to the farm, and none at all at this hour.

Not having any kind of weapon in the house, Laughlin lifted the poker from in front of the fire. It wasn't anything fancy, just a bar of iron that he had fashioned from some twisted steel bar that was lying around the place. It was warm to his touch. He found his powerful hand lamp in the dresser drawer, and went to the front door.

Outside, the clouds had come in and the place was pitch dark. He stood in the doorway and shone the powerful beam of light all around the yard, but could see no one. But he thought he heard a noise coming from the barn. He moved out across the yard towards the huge shed, and shone the light inside. Still, he could see nothing out of place.

"Who's there?" he said in as gruff a voice as he could muster.

There was no reply, so he advanced further into the darkness, and stepped inside the barn. As he did so, a shadowy figure emerged from beside the entrance.

"You won't grass on us again," the man said, and lunged forward, a knife held out in front of him. The steel entered Laughlin's side and went in deep. He dropped the lamp, and started to keel over. The assailant withdrew the blade, wiped it on Laughlin's clothes, and ran.

* * *

"Hello, Maureen?"

"Yes, Séan. Hi. What can I do for you?"

"I was just wondering if you've heard anything from Laughlin Faherty?"

"No, but I wasn't expecting to. Isn't he supposed to report in to you today?"

"Yes, that's just it you see. He hasn't come in, so I was wondering if he's been in touch with you maybe, looking for a day off or something."

"No, nothing this end. Why don't you ask Jim to go out to the farm and see what's going on? I hope he hasn't done a bunk."

"I doubt that. He's far too fond of that old place, and he has animals to tend to. But you are right, we need to find out what's going on. I'll send Jim out now."

"OK. Keep me posted, won't you?"

"Of course, Maureen. Catch you later."

When the call was ended, Mulholland summoned Jim Dolan and asked him to go out to the Faherty farm and see if there was any sign of Laughlin. If he found him there, he was to bring him in to the station in Clifden.

* * *

Dolan pulled the squad car into Faherty's yard and got out. He had a good look around, and could see no sign of life. He walked over to the old barn and looked inside, using the torch on his phone to illuminate the scene.

As he stood back, he noticed spots of blood on the concrete and a trail of blood drops leading back into the house.

He went into the house – the door was ajar – and found Laughlin Faherty slouched in the armchair in front of the fireplace, a large blood-soaked towel pressed against his side. Faherty was unconscious. Dolan went across to where the man was resting, not feeling very hopeful.

He held two fingers to Laughlin's neck and was pleased to find a pulse. He pulled out his mobile phone and called back to Clifden Garda station. When Mulholland got the call, he quickly phoned the ambulance that was based at the small hospital just down the road from the station and got the emergency call-out underway. Fifteen minutes later, the brightly coloured yellow and green ambulance pulled into the yard, and Jim Dolan went out to greet the paramedics.

"He's in here. He's alive but he's lost a lot of blood."

Faherty was attended by the two paramedics. The lad had been lucky, in a way. The fact that he had remained immobile in the same place had allowed his wound to close up a little, and although it had bled quite profusely at first, the blood soon coagulated and slowed to a modest weeping, before stopping altogether. The paramedics applied a dressing to ensure that it wouldn't start bleeding again, and they manhandled Laughlin onto a stretcher, getting him into the ambulance in short order. Telling Dolan that they were taking him to the small hospital on the outskirts of Clifden, they set off with the ambulance bouncing and swaying on the dirt track that led away from the house.

Dolan followed the vehicle into Clifden and, while they were unloading their damaged cargo, he called Séan Mulholland and brought him up to speed.

"What do you want me to do, Sarge?"

"Better stay with him for a while anyways. He may still be in danger and we don't want any fancy antics at the hospital. I'll give Galway a call and see what they suggest. OK?"

"Yes, Sarge, that's fine. Let me know what's happening later."

* * *

Almost as soon as Faherty had been transferred to a hospital bed, a young Indian doctor in a white coat with a stethoscope around his neck arrived and started to examine Laughlin. He was still unconscious, but the nurses had set up antibiotic and saline drips and connected various electronics up to him. A complicated-looking machine was beeping beside the bed, and the screen showed his heart rate to be sixty-five beats per minute.

When the doctor had finished his examination, Dolan approached him.

"How is he, doc?"

"He's a bit poorly, officer. He's lost a lot of blood, and we don't have any here to give him. There may be some serious internal injuries to his vital organs too. I'm going to have him transferred to the University Hospital in Galway

— they have proper equipment there, and more staff as well. He'll need an X-ray and a CT scan."

The doctor went off to make the arrangements, leaving Jim Dolan to look down on the man lying in the bed fighting for his life.

* * *

Séan Mulholland didn't like calling Lyons at this time of the night — by now it was nearly eleven o'clock — but he knew she liked to be kept informed of developments, so he decided to risk it.

He phoned her on her mobile and told her what had happened out at Boolagare.

"OK, Séan, thanks for letting me know. I'll get a uniformed officer out to the hospital to keep an eye on him when he gets there. I suspect the assailant hoped to do more damage to Laughlin than he actually managed. We don't want to give him the opportunity to finish the job. Thank Jim for me, won't you?"

"I will, to be sure, Maureen. We can talk again in the morning."

"Before you go, Séan, have you anyone out looking for the guy with the knife?"

"Well, as soon as I heard from Jim what had happened, I put out a message for the patrols to be on the lookout, but we have very little cover out here at night time, Maureen. There is one patrol car, but it has to cover hundreds of square miles, and in any case, it's based in Westport. So, I'd say the chances are pretty slim."

"Right, I see what you mean. Maybe I'll have a word with Mick and see if we can get some more resources out there. I'll get Sinéad out in the morning to the farm in any case to see if by any chance yer man left any traces, but I'm not hopeful."

"Right so. I'll bid you goodnight."

* * *

Laughlin Faherty's treatment continued through the night as soon as he arrived at Galway University Hospital. He was given adrenalin, a more powerful antibiotic and an anti-tetanus injection, and he was wheeled around to the various departments on his bed for X-ray and scans too. His blood was typed, and he was given a transfusion of two pints that took most of the night to administer. By morning, it had been established that none of his major organs had suffered from the wound, and with all the drugs, the replacement blood, and the care of the staff at the hospital, he was not only stable, but also coming out of unconsciousness.

"Look at you," the friendly auburn-haired nurse said as she did her final round before going off night duty. It was half past six in the morning.

"God, nurse, what happened? Where am I?"

"You're in Galway Hospital, and you were stabbed, Laughlin. But there's no lasting damage, though you'll be a bit sore for a few weeks. Would you like a cup of tea?"

"God, I would. My mouth is full of sand! Thanks."

"No bother. You just lie there and take it easy. I'll get you tea. Toast?"

"No thanks – just the tea."

Chapter Twenty-six

Lyons got everyone together early the following morning and told them of the adventures of Laughlin Faherty the previous night.

"Do you think it was the drugs crowd, boss?" Sally Fahy said.

"It could have been. I know they don't like anyone involved with them talking to the Guards. But I don't know. I have a feeling there's a lot more to this mining business than we know already. I'm going to see when we can go and interview Laughlin. I want to find out everything we can about the goings on with the exploration company. Eamon, will you call the hospital and find out when we can see him? Then we'll go together."

"What do you want me to do, boss?" Fahy asked.

"I want you to focus on the murder of Davin Faherty. We're not getting anywhere with that at all."

* * *

Superintendent Mick Hays recognised the number that was calling him on his mobile phone.

"Good morning, James. How's things?"

"Hello, Mick. I just thought I'd give you a call after you were asking about this stuff going on out west – you know, with the mining company."

"Oh, yes, thanks, what have you got?"

"Well, like all these things, it's complicated. It seems there may be a case of 'adverse possession' going on with quite a bit of the land out in the area you are interested in."

"Adverse possession – what in God's name is that?"

"It's a quirk of Irish land laws. If you are deemed to be in possession of land to which you have no legitimate title for a period, and the rightful owner has done nothing to correct the situation, then after a certain length of time you can claim legitimate title to the land. It's been used a few times over the past few years, but it's very controversial and problematic, but it's still on the statute book."

"I see. I didn't know about that. And who is claiming to own those lands now then?"

"Well, this is where it gets even quirkier. The claimants appear to be registered companies in places like Liechtenstein and the Cayman Islands."

"Bloody hell! Have you got any idea how widespread this is?"

"No, not really. But there seems to be quite a lot of land involved, and it also appears to coincide with the places where this mining crowd have expressed an interest."

"Right. I don't suppose you have the names of the companies making the claims?"

"Hang on, I did note a couple of them down somewhere. Yes, here we are. The one in Liechtenstein is called Company A900, which of itself is pretty peculiar. I haven't got the name of the Cayman one, but I could probably get it for you if it's important."

"No, it's OK, James, that's been really helpful, thanks. I'll follow it up from here."

"OK. Oh, and by the way, it's time to move on that apartment that you're interested in if you don't want it to slip away. There's a solicitor looking after it – Myles Dunne. Give him a call, he knows about your interest and he'll look after you."

"Oh, right. Thanks very much for all that, James. Send me a fee note for whatever we owe you."

"Ah, don't worry about it. We didn't have any outlay really."

"No, I insist, James. We have to be very careful about accepting favours these days. There's always some smartarse watching."

"I know what you mean. OK, then, I'll send a bill for €250, and you can buy me dinner some evening – how's that?"

"Terrific, thanks again."

When he had finished with James McMahon, Hays put a call through to the office of Myles Dunne and got speaking to the man himself.

"Oh, yes, James mentioned that you wanted to proceed with the purchase of the apartment down by the docks. I have all the paperwork prepared. If you could just drop me in a cheque for €57,500, I'll get working on transferring the title. In who's name do you want it?"

"Better put it in joint names of Ms Maureen Lyons and myself, Mr Dunne, and if you text me the bank details of your client account, I'll have my bank transfer the money across to you later today."

"Excellent. Many thanks, Superintendent. I'll confirm when it's all sorted out, and I'll text you the bank details now. What's your mobile number?"

Hays reeled off the number, and the solicitor took it down.

Hays rang down to Lyons' office when he had finished talking to the solicitor. He was dying to tell her the good news and pass on the information that James McMahon had dug up, but she didn't answer her phone.

* * *

Maureen Lyons arrived out at the city hospital just as lunch was being given to the patients. There was a strong smell of institutionally prepared food wafting through the corridors, and from observation, Lyons gleaned that it was brown stew that was being dished out, with mashed potato and peas.

Faherty was sitting up in the bed looking relatively well. His wound was hidden beneath the covers, so he looked as if there was nothing wrong with him as he reclined against the several pillows. His bed was covered in a pale blue cotton blanket. He was still attached to a beeping machine, but he appeared to be in quite good form as Lyons approached.

"Hello, Laughlin. How are you feeling today?" Lyons said.

"A lot better than yesterday, that's for sure. Did you catch the bugger who tried to see me off?"

"No, Laughlin, and without your help, it's very unlikely that we will," Lyons said, taking a seat on the rather basic plastic chair that was set beside Faherty's bed.

"So, tell me what happened then."

"I can't tell you nothing. I was in the house and I thought I heard a noise outside, so I went to see who was there. At first, I couldn't see anyone, so I went into the barn. Just as I got inside, the bugger came from my left and knifed me. Fecker."

"Did you get a look at his face at all?"

"No, he had a hoodie, and kept his head down, so I couldn't see him at all in the dark."

"Well, what can you tell us about him? Build? Height? How did he walk?"

"Jesus, I don't know. I was bloody stabbed, wasn't I? And it hurt like hell too, I can tell you. Still does."

"Where did he go after he knifed you, Laughlin?"

"How the hell should I know? He just ran off. It was pitch dark, and anyway I had collapsed on the floor. I was more worried about dying than whatever he was up to."

"Did you hear a vehicle start up, or anything?"

"No, I don't think so. But I can't be sure. Mind you, it was very still, so I would have heard if there was a car nearby."

"Is there anything else at all you can tell me about the incident, Laughlin?" Lyons said.

"No, sorry. Will you catch him, do you think?"

"Hard to say. We have almost nothing to go on. But we'll give it our best shot, don't worry."

Lyons left Laughlin to his meal, such as it was.

Lyons decided to drive out as far as Clifden to have a word with Séan Mulholland. He was a good man for local knowledge, and he might just hear something around the town that would help the Gardaí to identify the mystery assailant. On the way out in the car, she called back to Sally Fahy in Mill Street, to see if she had made any progress on the murder enquiry.

"Nothing new here, Inspector. How did you get on with Faherty?" Fahy said.

"Not very well. He couldn't tell me anything, so I'm on my way to Clifden to see Séan Mulholland. Maybe he'll be able to find out something. Anything else?"

"No. Oh, wait. Superintendent Hays was looking for you."

"OK, thanks, Sally. I'll give him a call. See you later."

The autumn weather had been kind to the land out along the N59. Dappled sunshine was breaking through the patchwork of white fluffy clouds, and here and there the reflections on the many large pools and small lakes on either side of the road made them look like silver, glistening in the sun. The heather had blossomed on the heathland too, with its vivid purple flowers providing a colourful carpet across the bogland.

Once she was past Oughterard, and the open road was more or less clear of traffic, although there were a few sheep grazing dangerously close to the edge of the road, Lyons used the hands-free system to call Mick Hays.

"Hi. You were looking for me," she said.

"Yes, I was. Where are you now?"

"I'm on my way out to Clifden to see Séan. I visited Laughlin Faherty in hospital, but he couldn't tell me anything about the assault. I'm hoping Séan may be able to tap the local grapevine and get something for us. What did you want me for?"

"It's nothing that can't wait. It's to do with your American mate, Gilbert. But I don't want to talk about it over the phone. Give me a call when you're back in town and I'll tell you then."

"Very mysterious, Superintendent. Pity you're not out here with me. The place is looking lovely today. We could go into Roundstone and partake of Mrs Vaughan's famous smoked salmon salad, I'm starving. Then we could have a walk down along Gurteen."

"Don't tempt me! Look, love, I'd better get on. These spreadsheets won't fill themselves in."

"They'd probably make more sense if they could, sir! I'll call you when I'm back. Love you."

"Love you too."

* * *

When Maureen Lyons reached the Garda station in Clifden, Sergeant Séan Mulholland was just settling down to his first cup of tea of the afternoon, accompanied by three chocolate Goldgrain biscuits.

"Ah, Maureen, come in. Can I get you a cup of tea?"

"Hi, Séan. Yes please, and I could do with a sandwich or something. I haven't eaten since breakfast."

"No bother. Jim will pop out and get you something from the deli down the street. Anything in particular you fancy?"

"No, just something tasty. Here's €10," she said, handing the note to Jim Dolan.

When Mulholland had poured her tea, and they were both seated in the office behind the front counter of the station, he said, "So, what brings you out here this fine autumn day?"

Lyons filled Mulholland in on the conversation with Laughlin Faherty in the hospital.

"'twas a bad business that. The poor fella could have been killed, and sure all he does is work that miserable place he likes to call a farm."

"Well, he had a bit of a side-line going too after Davin died. But listen, what I want to know is can we find the bloke with the blade, Séan? Have you heard anything down the pub or on the streets?"

"No, no I haven't. And I've been keeping my ear to the ground. But wait till I tell you. There is a family of ne'er-do-wells that live about two miles out the road. They're into everything, and we've had a couple of them for stealing stuff and brawling in the street here after the pubs close. I wouldn't put it past them to have something to do with it – or at least know something about it."

"What's the family name?"

"Callaghan. And there's one little bugger who's a bit out of control amongst them – Ian is his name. I could ask around and see if there's any word on what he's been up to lately, maybe drop out and see him sometime over the next few days. What do you think?"

"That's just what I was hoping for, Séan. Your local knowledge is really helpful in these cases. See what you can find out for me, will you?"

Just then Jim Dolan arrived back with a baguette packed with chicken and salad for Lyons, and gave it to her.

"Perfect, Jim, thanks a lot," she said, taking the first welcome bite of her belated lunch.

Chapter Twenty-seven

When Lyons got back to the station, she went straight to Hays' office. His personal assistant, Betty, was manning the desk outside his door as usual, and told Lyons to go on in.

"Hi. I'm back."

"So I see." He got up and went around the desk to give Lyons a hug and a quick kiss.

"You smell of fresh air. Have a nice time out west?"

"Fruitful, I'm hoping. Séan is a great man for a bit of nosing around out there. I'd say he'll have something for us in a day or two. Now, are you going to tell me your secrets?" she said with an impish smile as Hays went back behind his desk and sat down.

"Grab a seat. You'll enjoy this."

Hays went on to relate the information he had received. He outlined the fact that a peculiarity of Irish land law known as adverse possession had been used by some offshore companies to lay claim to some of the lands out near Boolagare.

"I wonder if our friend Gilbert has been involved in that?" Hays said.

"But that means he would have had to have started this some time ago – maybe years."

"Yes, it does. It's a slow burn, but if there is no registered owner of the land you are grabbing – if for example, it's common land – then that speeds up the process a lot. You only have to show that you are in possession of the place and that there is no one else with a claim, and Bob's your uncle. It can be done in a few years."

"God. Sounds right dodgy to me. Is this legit, this adverse possession?"

"There are some that believe it's against the constitution. Ireland has some pretty strong constitutional rights concerning land that stems from the time when we were occupied by the English. But no one has ever mounted a serious challenge in the courts, so it remains available to anyone who has the cheek to use it. Anyway, I've started turning over a few stones to see what we can find out about it. I'm using his former name too. If he's been plotting this for a few years, then some of the evidence trail may be in his old name."

"Who have you contacted?"

"It's rather a complex chain, to be honest. But it turns out we have some good contacts in the FBI. Finbarr apparently knows a few of them with ancestors that come from the same part of the country that he does, so they'd basically walk through hot coals for him. I looked up the FBI website too. One of their high priorities is to combat white collar crime, which I didn't know. I guess I've been watching too much *X-Files*. I thought they just went around shooting people and driving Ford Crown Victorias far too fast."

"Interesting. Maybe it's time for you and me to go to Castlerea and have a wee chat with our Mr Gilbert. What do you think?"

"Let's leave it till we hear back. Plunkett introduced me to a Special Agent O'Halloran. He's on the case now, and said he would get back to me with an update tomorrow. Seemed like a really nice man. Let's hope he gets something for us."

"OK. Gilbert isn't going anywhere for a while yet anyway."

"Oh, and by the way, I forgot to tell you, you are now the proud owner of number nine Claddagh Court, or at least half owner. I've paid over the money – or should I say, the bank has. We'll be getting the keys in the next few days. Now all we need is a tenant."

"That's great. Well done you! We'll have to go out and celebrate. And don't worry about a tenant. When I've seen the place and get some furniture into it, I'll put a notice up downstairs. There'll be a queue if we don't push the rent too hard."

"It wasn't any bother really. James McMahon was very helpful. He did most of it for me, to be truthful," Hays said.

"I hope that's OK, Mick. You know what they're like about accepting favours in this place these days."

"Don't worry, he's sending me a bill. I told him we needed to keep things above board, and he understands."

"You're not just a pretty face, are you, Superintendent?" she said, smiling at him.

"That's your job, sexy. Now go and leave me to the excitement of my quarterly spreadsheet on resource usage and performance against budget that has to be ready by tonight to send to Dublin."

"You get all the best jobs, Mick. Shall I book somewhere for later?"

"Oh, yes, do. Somewhere nice. Say seven-thirty. OK?"

"Yes, sir. See ya later."

* * *

Lyons had booked them into the Dela restaurant for dinner. It was just around the corner from the Garda station in Dominick Street, but being so close to home, as it were, they hadn't eaten there often.

Hays studied the menu, and praised Lyons for her choice of venue.

"This looks really good. I think I'll have the venison with game chips and a side of cherry sauce."

"I'm feeling fishy. I'll go for the monkfish in the orange and coconut sauce – sounds delicious."

They handed the menus back to the waiter as they placed their orders.

"This is a nice place, we should come here more often, Mick. It's so handy for the office too."

"Let's see what the food is like – though I've heard good reports. So, listen, how are things going with this Faherty case?"

"Not good, Mick. It's all so complicated. There's three or four things going on at once, and I have no idea if they all connect up in some crazy way. Have you any ideas?"

"I have some hope for that chap I was talking to in the US being able to throw some light on things. But surely Davin Faherty's death is nothing to do with the mining thing?" Hays said.

"That's just it. We've absolutely no clue whatever about that. No suspects, no clues, no useful forensics – nothing. All we know is that he was definitely bumped off, but I can't even see a motive in it for anyone."

"Didn't the brother say that Davin was against the whole idea of selling up to the mining company?"

"Yes, he did. But I can't see Gilbert being able to get hold of arsenic and managing to get the lad to ingest it. It doesn't make sense," Lyons said.

"Who found the body?"

"An old guy called Festus Greeley. I don't think he had anything to do with it. We did interview him, but he has no connection to any of the rest of the case. He's one of those old bachelors that never married and is just about managing a basic living from a few sheep out on the common."

"Do you know if he's sold out to the mining company?"

"I don't think we asked him that. The whole Derivest thing wasn't in the picture at that stage. But I seriously doubt if there's any connection."

Hays looked up from his meal and simply raised an eyebrow.

"I know what you're thinking, Mr Hays. The person who finds the body is often the culprit. But honestly, you need to meet this man. I can't believe he was in any way involved with it. But just to be on the safe side, I'll get Séan to have a bit of a root around – see if he can come up with anything."

"You'll have that poor man in an early grave – slave-driver!"

"Ah, away with ye. Séan enjoys a bit of action. It makes him feel important. And I'll tell you what, he's not half bad at the local stuff. I'm not saying you could write a procedures manual around his methods, but he does the business all the same. By the way, this fish is amazing. How's your venison?"

"Delicious. Really good. Yeah, to be honest I wish we had a few more like Mulholland in the force. Sometimes I think that the new, younger cops can't function without a PC and an iPhone."

"Well, let's see what tomorrow brings. Now, let's change the subject. I've had enough of this for today," Lyons said.

The two continued their meal with a sumptuous dessert followed by coffee. Both agreed that the meal had been excellent and vowed to return to the place sooner rather than later.

"That was great," Lyons said on the way back to the car park at the Garda station to collect their respective vehicles. They drove in convoy to their home in Salthill, arriving fifteen minutes later.

"Fancy a nightcap?" Hays said when they had settled indoors.

"Yeah, why not? It's not every day a girl adds to her property portfolio, after all. I hope we never fall out, Mick. It would be a father and mother of a job to disentangle that lot. Which reminds me, have I any legal interest in this place?"

"Oooohhh, look at you – this property thing is really going to your head. Brandy?"

"Yes, please," Lyons said.

"I'm not sure what the position is with cohabiting partners as far as property rights are concerned. Do you know anything about it?"

"Nope. Ah, don't worry about it. Just come here and show me how much you love me and we won't talk about breaking up – not tonight, anyway!"

Hays was happy to oblige.

Chapter Twenty-eight

Things were busy in Mill Street the following morning when Lyons arrived. As soon as she had settled in, she placed a call through to Clifden to speak to Séan Mulholland. The phone rang out ten times before Mulholland answered.

"Clifden Gardaí, Sergeant Mulholland speaking."

"Good morning, Séan, it's Maureen. I thought you'd gone AWOL there for a minute."

"Ah, not at all. I was just making a brew out the back. What ails you at this ungodly hour anyway?"

"You know that old-timer that found the body of Davin Faherty out at Shannalecka?"

"Yes, of course, Festus Greeley, he lives in an old thatched cottage well in off the road. What about him?"

"Superintendent Hays has asked if we can have a bit of a look at his background, and his circumstances – see if there's anything out of the ordinary."

"God, Maureen, you're grasping at straws. That man has lived out there all his life. He inherited the place when his mother died back in about 1990. He's well over seventy now, you know. What would your interest in him be?"

"It's just that he found the body, and Mick has a theory that it's always worth looking into the first person to come on the scene." Even as she was saying this, she realised that her partner's theory was very unlikely. "Well, just see what you can find out, Séan. We'll look like right eejits if there is a connection that we've missed."

"I presume you're getting nowhere with the investigation then?"

Lyons didn't respond.

"Anything else, Séan?" she said, keen to end the somewhat embarrassing conversation.

"There is, as it happens. You remember I was talking to you about the Callaghan family that live up there near the caravan park on the other side of Clifden?"

"Yes, what about them?"

"Well, the young fella I was curious about has done a runner. Gone. And the family are saying they don't know where he is. They say he just took off. He could be anywhere."

"Jesus, Séan, we're not doing very well, are we? Have you a photo of the guy. I can put out a person of interest notice."

"I haven't. But he drives, so I imagine he has a driving license. They should have a picture. I'll get the lads to keep their ear to the ground round and about too. I doubt if he's gone that far."

"Right, I'll get onto it so. Talk to you later, Séan. Thanks."

Lyons called John O'Connor in and gave him the details for Ian Callaghan, and asked him to see if he could get a photo from the National Driver License Service and circulate it.

Lyons then called Sally Fahy in.

"Sally, I want you and I to go through these three files and see what we've missed," she said when her colleague was seated across the desk from her.

"Three files! What three are those, boss?"

"There's the murder of Davin Faherty. This business with the mining company, and finally, the stabbing of Laughlin Faherty and his involvement with the drugs."

"Sounds like we'll need some coffee. What can I get you?" Fahy said.

"Good idea. I don't s'pose you'd nip across the road and get me a nice frothy cappuccino?"

"Course. Back in a mo."

While Fahy was gone, Lyons laid out the documents from the files on her desk, separated into three distinct piles. Fahy was back a few minutes later carrying two large cardboard cups of take-away coffee in a little tray and two blueberry muffins.

"God, you're an angel, Sally. Thanks."

"No problem, boss, what are we looking for?"

"A connection, a theme, anything that would help us to join the dots. I feel there's definitely something here – I just can't see it."

* * *

It was early afternoon when Hays heard back from Agent O'Halloran.

"Thanks for calling, Ethan. Have you managed to dig up anything on our friend?" Hays said.

"Hi, Mick. Yes, indeed I have. Quite a story you've unearthed there."

"Oh? You have my attention. What gives?"

"Your Mr Jed Gilbert was previously known as Jerome Gibson. As Gibson, he had quite a record. He'd been in jail. It looks like he's not a very nice type at all. Apparently, there were several other accusations against him before we got enough to put him away."

"Yes, we knew about his other name. Did you manage to get any information on what he's up to now?"

"Yeah, I did. I was here long into the night last night consulting all sorts. Thankfully, it's mostly online these days, so I didn't have to disturb anyone's beauty sleep. It looks as if your Mr Gilbert, or Gibson, has been planning this scam for a good few years. He set up a number of offshore companies, and they seem to have acquired title to lands in Ireland. Now, the odd thing is I can't trace any payment for the land – just some legal fees for registering the title, and a lot of gobbledegook about something called adverse possession, whatever that is."

"I see. How much land does he have now?"

"Not very much by US standards – just a few hundred acres. But that's not all. Recently, his offshore companies have sold on two parcels to a mining company."

"Don't tell me – Derivest, of Logan, Utah?" Hays said.

"Exactly right, Mick. And it looks like he did pretty well from the deal too. He got over fifty thousand US for each plot," Agent O'Halloran said.

"So, what would the whole thing be worth, do you reckon?"

"Close to a quarter of a million, I guess."

"Nice. If I've got this right then, it looks as if Gibson has somehow acquired this land for next to nothing, or absolutely nothing, and is selling it on to the mining company for big bucks," Hays said, picking up on the Americanisms.

"Yep, that's about it. But there's nothing illegal in any of that, as far as I can see."

"Maybe. What if he sold the land to Derivest on the basis that there are mineral reserves there, but in fact there aren't any minerals at all?" Hays said.

"I guess that would be a fraud. But surely the mining company would have the land surveyed?"

"Hmm. But if Gibson, or Gilbert was arranging the survey, and falsified the results to boost the price of the land, I presume that would be some sort of crime in the USA?"

"Hard to say without more information, Mick. The offshore thing complicates it, and it could be tricky to determine where exactly the crime, if any, occurred. Do you want me to keep digging?"

"No, it's OK for now, Ethan. That's fantastically helpful, thank you. I'll get back to you if we need more. And, of course, I'll keep you up to date with any developments from this end."

* * *

When Mick Hays had finished talking to Agent O'Halloran, he went looking for Lyons. She was still in her office with Sally Fahy, pouring over the files trying to forge a link between the events of the past few weeks.

"Sorry to disturb you, ladies, but you need to hear this," Hays said, coming and sitting down beside Sally Fahy across the desk from his partner.

"Shall I go?" Fahy said, concerned that the information about to be revealed was above her pay grade.

"No, not at all. This may be just what both of you are looking for," Hays said.

He recounted what the American officer had told him about Gilbert's business affairs, much to the amazement of the two women who listened intently until he was finished.

"Crikey. And do you think there's any connection to Davin Faherty's murder, sir?" Fahy asked.

"It seems Davin was very much against selling out to the mining company – or so his brother told us. Maybe Gilbert needed to have him removed in order to do the deal with Laughlin," Lyons suggested.

"It seems a bit extreme to me. And how would he have arranged it? You can't exactly put up a card in the post office looking for someone to commit murder."

"Yes, but he has form for violence," Lyons said, keen not to have her idea dismissed at once.

"OK, but where would he get arsenic, and how would he have administered it?" Hays pressed on.

"Well, he didn't have much trouble drugging Mary Fallon, did he?" Hays said.

"True. But there's a difference between slipping a girl a Mickey Finn and killing someone with arsenic and dumping them in the bog," Hays said.

"So, what are we going to do now?" Sally Fahy asked.

"I think you two need to get up to Castlerea and have a word with Gilbert. Lay it on good and thick. Put the wind up him. See if you can break him. I'm going to talk to his boss in Utah. It might be time for him to come and visit his land in Ireland, I'm thinking."

"Good idea. We'll get up there this afternoon. Let me know what happens with Mr Deri, won't you?"

"Yes, of course."

Chapter Twenty-nine

"Good morning, Mr Deri. This is Superintendent Michael Hays from the Galway police. Have you got a minute?" Hays said when he finally got through to the American after a good degree of obfuscation by Deri's secretary.

"Hi, Inspector, what can I do for you today?"

"As you know, Mr Deri, we have been investigating a number of serious crimes here in Ireland in which one of your employees appears to be entangled – a Mr Jed Gilbert, formerly known as Jerome Gibson."

"Now hold on a minute, Inspector. Firstly, Jed Gilbert is not exactly an employee of mine – he's an associate that works for us on the initial stages of some of our explorations. And I have no idea what you mean by formerly known as. What in hell is all that about?"

"Well, Mr Deri, your Mr Gilbert has quite a past. I presume you are aware that he has a criminal record, and has done jail time?"

"Look, Superintendent, I'm sure you mean well, but this is nonsense. Gilbert is one of the most honest people I know. You've got it wrong, wherever you got your information."

"I got my information from a special agent in the FBI, Mr Deri. Of course, they may be mistaken, but I somehow doubt it."

Deri wasn't expecting that. He went silent for several moments.

"Mr Deri, we have also discovered that Mr Gilbert may have been involved in falsifying the reports that you received about minerals on lands in the west of Ireland, and on which basis your company made various purchases. I think it might be well worth your while taking a trip over here to see if we can't get this whole mess sorted out."

"I see. Can you tell me more?"

"I'm not comfortable discussing the matter further on the phone, Mr Deri. But if you decide to come here, I'll be happy to lay out all that we have found for you. It's not a pretty picture."

"Hmm... OK. Look, I need to talk this over with some of my people here. Why don't I call you later and let you know what's been decided?"

"Yes, OK. But remember the time difference. Your time is seven hours behind us – so please don't call me after 3:00 p.m. local time. Here's my personal cell number," Hays said, reciting his mobile number complete with the +353 international code.

* * *

On the drive to Castlerea, Lyons received a call from Sinéad Loughran.

"Hi, Sinéad. What's the story?"

"I have some more information about the death of Davin Faherty. Let me see now. Yes, here it is. I sent a blood sample off to the University lab in Dublin to see if they could tell us anything more about the poison that Davin died from. They love doing some real analysis on live cases."

"And?" Lyons said, a little impatient to hear what had been discovered, if anything.

"Interesting. The substance used to poison him was an arsenic compound as we suspected, but it was a component of rat poison. It must be pretty old too. They don't use arsenic in rat poison these days, it's too toxic."

"Rat poison – yuck! I don't suppose they could be specific about the brand?"

"No, nothing like that. Just that it had other ingredients with it that points to rat poison. I have the full details here is a report. I'll email it on to you."

"Thanks, Sinéad. I'm on the road to Castlerea just now, but I should be back in the office later on. See ya."

When the call had ended, Fahy said to Lyons, "I wonder if our Mr Gilbert has a little stash of rat poison among his stuff?"

"Hmm, I guess he could have. If Davin was blocking his acquisition of the Faherty lands, as his brother says he may have been, then he could have had something to do with the murder. I have no idea how he might have engineered it, but it gives something else to talk to him about in any case!"

"Doesn't it just!" Fahy said.

* * *

When they arrived at the Castlerea remand centre, there was quite a lot of procedure to go through before they could actually get to speak to Jed Gilbert. After just over half an hour, they were shown into a room sparsely furnished with just a table and some chairs, all of which were fixed to the floor. A uniformed officer stood at the back of the room near the door with his hands folded behind him.

As soon as the two detectives entered the room, Gilbert started remonstrating.

"You know, Inspector, you have absolutely no right to keep me here. I am an American citizen, and I have rights. This is going to cause you a great deal of trouble. I'll have your badge for this."

"Relax, Mr Gilbert. The American embassy have been fully informed of your presence here, and to be honest, they are not in the least concerned. In fact, they suggested that if we kept you here for the rest of your life, they wouldn't be that bothered," Lyons said, taking her seat in the somewhat uncomfortable plastic chair.

"You're lying, Inspector. I'm known to the authorities in the USA. What you're saying is just not credible."

Lyons looked at Fahy, signalling her to take up the conversation.

"Yes, Mr Gilbert, we understand you are indeed known to the US authorities. An FBI agent has confirmed your criminal record to us. So, we'd like to ask you a few questions, and it would be in your interests to answer honestly."

"I've nothing to hide," Gilbert said sullenly.

"Good, then let's get on. Now, what can you tell us about your business interests in offshore companies that have been grabbing land in the west of Ireland?" Lyons asked.

"I don't know what you're talking about."

"I'm talking about the fact that you are the sole proprietor of a number of companies that have been acquiring lands in the west of Ireland using some rather dubious techniques."

"In your dreams."

Lyons took another piece of paper from her folder. She turned it around for Gilbert to look at. The document was the registration document for Company A900 and showed Jerome Gibson as the only owner.

Gilbert just shrugged.

"Let me tell you what I think, Mr Gilbert. I think you set this scam up some time ago. You acquired the land using the adverse possession instrument that you came across in Irish law. Then you sat on the land for a while before inventing the possibility of mineral wealth, and sold the idea to Derivest. We know you have disposed of at least two parcels of the stolen land to Derivest for a lot of money. So why don't you tell us the rest of the story?"

"This is all bullshit. You can't prove any of this."

"Oh, I think we probably can, Mr Gilbert. And once we contact Chuck Deri and have a nice close look at the soil analysis you invented to fool him, I think you'll be surprised at what comes to light. We're not finished with you at all yet!" Lyons said.

For the next few minutes an uneasy silence filled the room. Then Fahy took another tack.

"Mr Gilbert, we know that you have access to drugs – after all, you managed to dose Mary Fallon's drink with Rohypnol. What other illicit substances do you keep amongst your things?"

"I don't know what you mean."

"What about arsenic, or rat poison?"

"Jesus, woman, you've been reading too many whacky crime novels! For the record, I've got no idea what you are talking about."

Fahy was not going to be put off that easily.

"OK. Then let me paint you a picture. Your little wheeze with the adverse possession wouldn't have worked with the Faherty land. They have legitimate rights to that land, and they are using it all the time, so any attempt on those lines would fail. But you needed their land to complete the claim for Derivest. Now we know that Davin Faherty was not in favour of selling out, and now he's mysteriously dead. For your information, he was poisoned with arsenic. So, given your propensity for administering illegal substances to innocent folks, we join the dots and what have we got?"

"Oh, now, wait a minute. You can't pin the death of Davin Faherty on me. I had nothing to do with that at all."

"Really? It looks like a bit more than just a coincidence to me. And you have form. You know what they say – motive, opportunity and means – and it looks to me as if you had all three."

Gilbert was clearly very agitated at the prospect of being charged with murder. He wasn't sure if they still had the death penalty in Ireland, and while he felt probably not, he was now genuinely scared that the Gardaí would manage to connect him to the death of Davin Faherty.

"Look, I'm ready to admit to giving that little tease Mary, or whatever her name is, a little something to relax her a bit. But I'm definitely not coughing for anything to do with homicide. No, ma'am. Not on your life."

"What about the land scams, Jed?"

"There's nothing illegal in that. It was all above board — you know how it works."

"But when it comes out that there's no sign of any minerals on the land, and that you falsified the soil analysis reports, then it shows that the whole thing was just one big fraud. That will negate all those transactions, and you'll have to pay Deri back whatever he paid you for the two plots that Derivest bought from you. Of course, there will be further charges arising too."

Gilbert leant forward and put his head in his hands.

"That's it. I'm not saying nothing more. I'm done," he muttered dejectedly.

Lyons looked at Fahy and nodded to her.

"Right, as you wish. We'll be in touch, Mr Gilbert."

Chapter Thirty

Chuck Deri followed the same route as Jed Gilbert had in order to get himself from Logan, Utah to Shannon Airport. It was exhausting, and throughout the journey, during which Deri didn't sleep at all, he tried in vain to process what Superintendent Hays had told him.

Before he left the office, he collected up all the documents he could easily lay his hands on pertaining to his company's interests in the exploration in the west of Ireland. He included the reports that Gilbert had furnished showing that there were considerable deposits of valuable minerals in the ground all around the area. He didn't have time to check the veracity of the reports before leaving, as to do so would have made him miss the flight from Newark to Shannon.

United Airlines had put a Boeing 757 on the route this particular evening. The 757 is a narrow-bodied aircraft, originally designed to serve busy city pairs in the United States and Europe, but had been pressed into longer haul work as Extended Twin Operations became fashionable in the 1990s on routes where the loads didn't warrant a larger machine.

Chuck Deri was a big man. Even though the airline had made the business class seats a good deal wider than those in coach, he barely fitted into it, and he spent a very uncomfortable and largely sleepless night squirming around trying to get comfortable as the airliner pressed on eastwards through the darkness toward Europe. Thankfully, there was very little turbulence on the route that evening, so after what seemed like an eternity, the cabin lights were put back on and breakfast was served as the plane was forty-five minutes out from Shannon. As he finished his food and his tray was being cleared, he got the first glimpse of the green fields of Counties Limerick and Clare as the flight descended through the misty clouds in the early morning dawn.

Hays had arranged for Deri to be met on arrival by plain clothes officers from Limerick, and they stood outside in arrivals with a white card bearing the name Mr Chuck Deri. When Deri emerged, introductions were completed and all three set off for Galway. The two Gardaí asked Deri if he needed to stop for food or refreshment along the way, but he declined their offer, saying that he had breakfasted on the flight. At just after eight o'clock in the morning, the car pulled into the yard at the side of Mill Street Garda station and Deri went inside.

Hays had been expecting the early arrival, and both he and Lyons were already in the station. Hays went to the front desk to greet their visitor, again asking if there was anything that he needed, before bringing him upstairs to Hays' own comfortable office.

"Many thanks for making the trip across, Mr Deri. I thought it was best to ask you to come here based on the information that we have uncovered about the activities of Mr Gilbert," Hays said as the three of them were seated around Hays' mahogany desk.

"Yeah, Superintendent, I'm intrigued to be honest. You know I'm the third generation of Deris to run our little outfit, and we've always been scrupulously honest and straight with everyone we have dealt with. It comes from my family's Welsh Presbyterian background. So if there's been any funny business going on, I want to get to the bottom of it, and make it right for anyone who has been adversely affected."

Hays thought that the man was being a little too gracious for a hard-nosed American businessman, but he was prepared to give him the benefit of the doubt – for now.

Hays spent twenty minutes explaining to Chuck Deri all that they had discovered about Jed Gilbert's activities around Connemara while Deri and Lyons stayed silent. When he had finished, the American spoke up.

"Well, firstly, Superintendent, let's look at the soil analysis that Jed had done. We use Clandillon Geological Data Services based in Bristol, UK for this kind of thing. They are a small outfit specializing in terrestrial mining. So many of the big guys have turned to marine geology – that's where the money is these days. I have their reports here."

Deri reached into his bag and took out a cream-coloured folder in which several sheets of paper had been pinned. Hays, reading upside down, could make out the logo and name of Clandillon at the top of the first page.

Deri turned the folder around for Hays to read. The report, which included a map of the area around Boolagare, Shannalecka, and lands stretching across to Murvey and Dog's Bay, was quite technical and described the tests used on a number of core samples to determine the presence of recoverable minerals. pH appeared several times, along with some complicated geological terms and processes that Hays didn't understand. He turned to the end of the report where conclusions were listed, and read that in the opinion of Clandillon's experts, there were indeed recoverable quantities of copper and gold present in the samples presented, along with a number of disclaimers stating that the analysis was based on the material provided only, and that any extrapolation of the results was not the responsibility of the analysts.

"What does this signal to you, Mr Deri? To be truthful, I don't really understand much of the report, except that the conclusion appears positive," Hays said.

"On the basis of that report, Derivest would certainly want to move to the next stage, Superintendent."

"And what exactly would that entail?"

"We would open up a test mine in the most promising area. We'd bring in a team and some machinery and extract a few tons of material and see what it contained. We have portable sluices and crushers for that job, and then we'd take the raw ore off to a smelter somewhere and determine the mineral content before going at it full steam ahead."

"And do you have to own the land that you are mining, Mr Deri?" Lyons asked.

"That's usually how it works, yes. We have made a number of purchases in the area at very generous rates, if I may say so. That land is no good for anything really, so the local farmers will do very well from our endeavours."

"OK, then. Here's what I'd like to do. Maureen, can you take Mr Deri down to your office and introduce him to Jerome Gibson? Show him the information we have on Gibson's off-shore businesses too. I'm going to wait till after nine o'clock and call Clandillon in Bristol to verify these reports. I presume you haven't already done that, Mr Deri?"

"No, of course not. As I said, we have used them previously. They are totally reliable."

"Right, well if you'll excuse me, I'll see you later," Hays said.

Lyons and Deri got up and went down to her office where Deri was pleased to accept a cup of strong coffee and a Danish pastry that Sally Fahy had procured from the local Starbucks.

* * *

"Clandillon Geological, how may I help you?" a young woman's voice said when Hays rang the company at quarter past nine.

"Good morning. I wonder if I could speak to the person who handles the Derivest work please?" Hays said.

"Just a moment, sir. That would be Mr Malcolm Clandillon. I'll see if he's free. Who shall I say?"

"Hays, Michael Hays. I'm calling from Ireland."

The phone went onto some banal lift music for a few moments, and then a man with an educated British accent answered.

"Malcolm Clandillon. How can I help you, Mr Hays?"

"Actually, it's Superintendent Hays from the Galway police, Mr Clandillon. I wonder if I could ask you to authenticate a geological survey report that has come up in an investigation we are carrying out?"

"Well, yes, I suppose so. Have you got it there?"

"Yes, I have. There's a folio number on the top of the first page – just a sec – it's IRE/3479. Does that help?"

"Yes, I'll just look that up in our system. Hold on a moment please."

Hays could hear the man typing on a keyboard, and the click of a mouse.

"No, I'm sorry, Superintendent, there is no such reference in our system. The format is correct, but we have never used that particular folio number. Our references only go as far as 2245."

"I see. So, what you are telling me is that this report did not originate with your company, is that correct, even though it appears to be on Clandillon letterhead."

"Well, that reference number simply doesn't exist. But I would obviously be concerned if someone is faking our stationery. Can you tell me any more about it?" Clandillon said.

"Have you ever done any work for a Mr Gilbert from Derivest, Mr Clandillon?"

"Oh, yes. We have. Quite a bit actually."

"Could I ask you to look up your system again and see if he ever submitted soil samples from the west of Ireland for analysis – say in the last twelve months?"

"Yes, all right. Just hold on again please."

The keyboard was back in action, along with the mouse.

"Mr Hays. Yes, we did a report for Mr Gilbert recently on soil cores in that area. Why do you ask?"

"Could you have a quick look at the report for me and tell me if there were any mineral deposits found as a result of your analysis?"

"Just a second."

Hays could hear more keys being tapped on the man's computer keyboard.

"Those reports were all negative, Mr Hays. There were no minerals or mineral indicators found. There were some arsenic traces in the soil, but when analysed, it turns out that they were due to extensive peat deposits in the area. Nothing to do with minerals. May I ask what all this is about, Superintendent?"

"Ongoing enquiries, Mr Clandillon. I doubt that your company will be implicated if it comes to anything, though. What you have told me points fairly obviously at forgery of some kind. But I'll let you know the outcome in due course," Hays said.

"Should we be... eh... how shall I say it, cautious in our dealings with Derivest and Mr Gilbert in future, Superintendent?"

"I doubt if you'll be hearing from Gilbert for quite a while, but there's nothing that we have discovered so far that would implicate Derivest in any wrongdoing."

"Very well. Thank you for that, Superintendent. Be sure to let me know what develops if you'd be so kind."

"I will, and thanks for your help."

Chapter Thirty-one

Garda John O'Connor called across the open plan to Sally Fahy, who was seated at her desk sipping a cup of take-away coffee.

"Sarge, there's an Inspector O'Higgins on the phone for you."

"Thanks, John. I'll take it here," she said.

"Good morning, Inspector. How can I help?"

"Hello, Sally. I just wanted to let you know what's going on with Laughlin Faherty and the drugs thing. Faherty won't tell us who the organisers of the grow house are, or anything else about the operation, so I want to turn the heat up on him a bit. I know he's been let off with a caution, but I'm interested in who is behind the whole thing."

"OK. That sounds like a good idea. What have you in mind?" Fahy said.

"He's back home now. He was discharged from hospital – it seems his sheep need him! I've organised a search warrant for his place. It's been issued on the basis that he may be storing some of the finished product ready for distribution on his farm. I don't think he is, but it will shake him up a bit if we turn the place over and it might loosen his tongue. So far, he isn't really taking his position seriously," O'Higgins said.

"Yeah, I see what you mean. After all, he's still at liberty, and doing much the same as before we caught him, so he may well think he's gotten away with it."

"Exactly. I was wondering if you'd like to help us with the search? After all you were there for the arrest, and you never know, we might just find something incriminating out at his place," O'Higgins said.

"Yeah, sure. But I'd need to clear it with my boss here first. When are you planning to execute the search warrant?"

"I thought tomorrow early doors would be best – say around six o'clock. I know it's early, but in my experience these things go best in the early morning when the suspect is bleary-eyed. I'll get three or four uniformed Gardaí from here to help out. Oh, and don't worry about clearing it with Maureen – I'll look after that."

"Thanks. So, what are the arrangements?"

"We'll meet at Clifden Garda station at 5:30 a.m. for a briefing. I'll get Sergeant Mulholland to have the place open for us. Then we go out to Boolagare and serve the warrant on Faherty and conduct the search. It will take a while, because the warrant covers the whole place – cottage, barn, all the outhouses and so on. But we should be finished by lunchtime. Does that sound OK to you?"

"Yes, perfect, Inspector. See you tomorrow at 5:30 then."

"Great. Thanks, Sally. See ya."

* * *

It was a chilly morning, but mercifully dry, when the Gardaí arrived outside Clifden Garda station just before half past five the following morning. Fahy had discussed the operation with Lyons the previous afternoon, and had asked Lyons if she thought that she should bring a firearm. Lyons said no, but told her to make sure to bring her self-defence spray and her retractable baton, just in case.

Sergeant Séan Mulholland had come down at five o'clock to open the Garda station himself on this occasion, and by half past five he had the heating fired up and a large teapot full of strong tea and the inevitable packet of chocolate Goldgrain biscuits all laid out for the troops, for which they were very grateful.

When they were all gathered, O'Higgins commenced the briefing.

"OK, listen up, folks. This is largely just a show of intent on our part. I don't really think that we'll find a large stash of drugs but you never know. We need to be thorough. Search everywhere – in drawers, cupboards, under the beds, open tins, boxes and containers as much as you like – let's put on a good show for Mr Faherty.

Sally, can you take Cathal here and do the barn," O'Higgins said, pointing to a young, tall, thin Garda with a ruddy complexion.

"Then if you have time, have a look in the other outhouses too. I'll take the house with Brian and Tom here. If anyone finds anything, leave it in situ and call me immediately. We need to get photographs of whatever it is. Oh, and be sure to wear vinyl gloves and shoe protectors too. If nothing else, it looks more intimidating. Right, any questions?"

"Sir. What do we do with Faherty while this is going on?" Tom asked.

"Good question, Tom. He's entitled to be present, but not to obstruct us. But after that he can do what he likes."

"What if he tries to leave?" Tom persisted.

"He won't. They never do, especially if there is anything there to be found. I'll keep him busy anyway, and I'll be watching for his blood pressure to rise if we get close to anything illegal stashed around the place. OK, everyone, finish your tea and let's go. Thanks, Séan, for opening up for us, and the refreshments."

Mulholland looked wistfully at the few crumbs left on the empty plate which had, a few minutes earlier, held a full packet of his favourite biscuits.

"You're welcome, sir. Glad to be of help."

* * *

The convoy of three vehicles, one of which was a marked Garda car, swung into the yard at Faherty's place at almost exactly six o'clock. For effect, the blue lights on the squad car had been turned on for the last few yards of the journey, and the old cottage and the damp concrete yard were illuminated in an eerie glow as a result.

O'Higgins got out of his car and went to the front of the house where he thumped hard three times on the wooden door. A few seconds later, he repeated the exercise, this time shouting in a loud voice, "Police – open up."

They waited patiently, and after a minute or two the door opened, revealing a dishevelled-looking Laughlin Faherty dressed in a plaid dressing gown over striped cotton pyjamas.

"Christ! What the fuck do you lot want? Don't you know what time it is?" he croaked, still half asleep.

"Mr Faherty, we have a warrant to search these premises," O'Higgins said, holding up the paper for the occupant to peruse if he so wished, "we believe there may be prohibited substances or the paraphernalia for same being stored here. Now please stand aside and let my officers carry out their duties."

Faherty stood aside as O'Higgins and his two colleagues went into the house.

"This is crazy. There are no drugs here, and you have no right to come barging into private property at this ungodly hour. I'm going to make a complaint about this – wait till you see."

O'Higgins ignored Faherty's protestations – he had heard the same threat many times previously.

"Why don't we sit down and have a chat, Laughlin, and let these officers get on with their work?"

Faherty said nothing but moved across to the well-scrubbed wooden table in the middle of the room and sat down.

Outside, Cathal pushed back the rusty iron door on the barn and invited Sally Fahy to go in ahead of him. She found a light switch, and four single fluorescent tubes suspended from the ceiling on chains started flickering to life, as if they too had been woken from a deep slumber. They cast a dim light on the old barn with its ancient tractor parked on the floor in the centre of the large shed.

All down along one side of the barn there were wooden shelves and a makeshift workbench with a big vice attached to one end. The shelves were packed with tins, bottles and boxes of stuff – mostly oils and greases used to keep farm machinery working, and some more obscure packets of stuff that Fahy didn't recognise.

She shone her torch along the shelves and stopped with it shining on an old glass oil bottle a third full with a greeny-brown viscous liquid. She could see something behind the bottle, and when she moved it out of the way, her torch illuminated an old cardboard drum about the size of a tub of Bisto, or drinking chocolate. She reached up and took out the red and yellow container, shining the torch on the label which read 'Endorats' in a font that looked to be straight out of the 1960s and with a picture of a rodent on the front in black and white. The lid of the container was rusty, but she prised it open with her fingernails, revealing that it was half full of a cream-coloured powder. It looked as if a scoop or two had been recently removed, because while much of the contents was caked and dark in colour, a section in the centre was paler and looked fresher. Fahy put the lid back on the tub and took out a plastic evidence bag from her jacket, placing the container carefully inside so as not to further disturb the contents.

"I need to talk to the inspector, Cathal. Can you carry on here?"

"Yes, sure. There doesn't seem to be anything here anyway, but I'll finish it off and then have a look in the other building in the yard."

Fahy called O'Higgins outside and told him what she had found in the barn.

"If it's OK with you, sir, I'd like to take this back to Sinéad Loughran in the lab and have it analysed. And maybe we shouldn't tell Faherty what I'm doing just yet – what do you think?"

"Good idea. You head off. We'll finish up here. Faherty's still not talking, but I haven't finished with him yet."

"OK, thanks."

As Sally Fahy drove back to Galway, despite the early hour, she called Maureen Lyons to provide an update.

"Wow! Well done you. I'll give Sinéad a call in a while and tell her to expect you. This could be significant."

Chapter Thirty-two

"Come in, Mick; Maureen. Sit ye down," Chief Superintendent Finbarr Plunkett said. He had summoned them to his office to discuss the ongoing case, and was obviously uneasy about something.

"Can I get you some tea or coffee?" he said.

"Tea would be lovely – thanks, sir," Lyons said and Hays nodded.

Plunkett used the intercom on his desk to make the arrangements, and then turned to Hays.

"I need a candid appraisal of where we are with this whole Faherty thing. I've had yer man from Utah bending my ear, and I'm concerned he might get a bit of traction with that lot up in Dublin and cause us all kinds of grief. What's going on?"

Hays outlined what they knew of the Faherty killing, and the possibility of links to the mineral exploration. He also filled his boss in on the antics of Jed Gilbert in terms of his assault on Mary Fallon, and his previous history of violence.

"Have we anything that actually ties Faherty's death in with the mining, Mick?"

"Not specifically. We know the lad that died was against selling their land to Derivest, while the brother appears to have been in favour. We can't establish if there was a serious row between them – the brother isn't very talkative," Hays said.

"But we have him on some drugs charges, as I understand it. Can you not use that to loosen his tongue? And I hear there was an attempt on his life too. Surely he'll come clean," Plunkett said.

"There is something else, sir. Sorry, Mick, I haven't had time to share this with you. Sergeant Fahy has been out to the farm with Inspector O'Higgins and they carried out a search of the place. They found some old rat poison in the barn that looked as if it had been disturbed recently. It's on its way for analysis now, sir."

"God! What next?" Plunkett said.

"What exactly is Mr Deri complaining about, sir?" Hays asked.

"Ah, you know, the usual crap about American citizens – their rights, freedom – all that baloney that they usually go on with. He wants Gilbert to be allowed to return to Utah. He says they'll deal with him over there. I presume you've been in touch with the embassy about Gilbert?"

"Yes, sir, we have. Basically, they have no interest in him," Lyons said.

"And what exactly have you charged him with?" Plunkett said.

"Assaulting a member of the Garda, sir. He's been remanded to Castlerea," Lyons said.

"Is that all? What about all this malarkey with the land and the bogus analysis?"

"That's more complicated, sir. It's actually quite hard to determine where exactly the fraud took place. The land transactions were all arranged offshore, and the false soil analysis was more than likely prepared when Gilbert was in the USA. I noticed the actual report was on letter-sized paper. If it had been done here or in the UK it would have been on A4 paper," Lyons said.

"And did this fella Chuck not spot that?" Plunkett said.

"Apparently not, sir."

"Huh, some genius he is. So, what I'm hearing is that we could send Gilbert packing with a slap on the wrist if we wanted to. I'm sure Mary Fallon would be glad to see the back of him."

"Well, I'd like to be one hundred percent certain that he didn't have a hand in the death of Davin Faherty, or the assault on the brother before we let him go. But I agree, the assault on Mary could be handled with a caution. She didn't actually come to any real harm."

"Have we made contact with law enforcement in the States about Gilbert?" Plunkett said.

"Yes, sir. I've been in contact with that agent O'Halloran from the FBI. It was he who gave me the information linking Gilbert to the offshore companies that acquired land using the adverse possession instrument to sell back to Derivest. O'Halloran's a really nice guy – Irish roots of course."

"OK. Well, here's the plan," Plunkett said, pausing while Betty brought in a tray of refreshments for them all and set it down.

* * *

When Lyons got back down to her desk, there was a message for her to call Sinéad Loughran. After leaving Plunkett's office, Hays and Lyons had discussed how exactly they would execute the plan, and had made some decisions.

They had sent a van up to Castlerea to collect Gilbert and bring him back down to Mill Street where Hays himself was going to question the man. Hays reckoned that he could get Gilbert to talk and tell him the extent of his involvement in what had been going on.

Meanwhile, Lyons called the forensic lab and spoke to Sinéad.

"Hi, Sinéad, you were looking for me."

"Yes, thanks for calling back, Maureen. Sally dropped off an old tub of rat poison here earlier on. She asked me to analyse it, and well, I did."

"And…?"

"Sally was right. Some of the powder has been removed recently. Furthermore, the poison contains significant amounts of arsenic, and I'm having a detailed tox report drawn up to see if it matches the poison we found in Davin Faherty's body," Loughran said.

"And if you were a gambling girl, Sinéad?"

"I'd give you ten to one that we'll get a match. These old compounds are very straightforward. There will be traces of the nicer stuff that they put in there to attract the rodents that will have been present in Faherty's system. We may not get a 100% match on it, but there'll be enough to stand up in court if it comes to that."

"Any prints on the container?"

"Yep. Just Laughlin Faherty's. We had his prints from when he was arrested for the drugs thing, and they're a perfect match. I got them from the metal lid."

"OK, great, that'll do me. I'll get Seán to send someone out to Boolagare to lift Laughlin and bring him in. Let's see what he has to say for himself."

* * *

It was late afternoon by the time Hays got the call to say that Jed Gilbert was downstairs in an interview room. He went down immediately, removing his tie first and leaving it in his office, and rolling up his shirt sleeves so that he looked a bit rougher than usual. He finished the look by tussling up his hair.

When he went into the interview room, he sat down opposite Gilbert and put a thick Manila folder on the table.

"Now, Mr Gilbert, you and I are going to have a little one-to-one, and I should tell you I've had a bitch of a day and I'm in a very bad mood, so don't piss me off!"

Gilbert was startled at the outburst, and tried to move back from the table, but his chair was fixed to the ground.

"Guard, why don't you go and see if you can get me a cup of tea, and take your time now, won't you," Hays said to the uniformed Garda that had been standing by the door with his arms behind his back.

The officer departed leaving the two of them alone in the office.

"Shouldn't you be recording this?" Gilbert said, nodding at the tape recorder at the side of the table.

"Ah, we won't worry too much about that, Mr Gilbert. Now, this is the story," Hays said leaning in towards Gilbert and lowering his voice.

"I've dealt with worse than you in my time, I can tell you. And there's something you need to know about the position you're in. We're a small force here in Galway, and we sometimes find that conventional policing methods are a bit – how shall we say – inappropriate. So occasionally, we throw away the manual and make it up as we go along. Do you get my drift?"

"So, what do you want from me?"

"I want you to tell me all you know about the fraud you have been carrying out with the land out in the west, and everything you know about the death of Davin Faherty. And before you start, let me tell you what might happen if I'm not satisfied with your answers. You see, sometimes men like you just disappear. That's right – gone – never to be seen or heard of again. No one would miss you. The US embassy don't give a damn about you. Chuck Deri wants to wring your neck, and well, we aren't too pleased with that stunt you pulled on Mary Fallon either. So, you're a long way from home, and you have no friends here. If you just weren't around anymore, who would care? See what I mean?"

"Are you threatening me?" Gilbert said.

"Damn right, I am. But it's not just idle threats, Mr Gilbert. You wouldn't be the first prisoner we have 'lost' between here and Castlerea. And you needn't bother with all that crap about being an American citizen and your rights – just now, you don't have any. So, start talking, and make it good."

What Hays said about losing prisoners wasn't true of course, but Gilbert didn't know that.

Jed Gilbert only had to think for a few seconds before realising that there was only one sensible course of action to take. He told Hays everything that he had been involved in. How he had set it up years ago when he read an article in the paper about possible mineral deposits in the west of Ireland. He registered a number of offshore companies and started researching land titles in the area. He came across an incidence of adverse possession that had been featured when a local personality had used it to acquire some land in Dublin's leafy suburbs.

Then he worked on getting a position with Derivest. He changed his name, and endeared himself to Chuck Deri who gave him a job in the company. After that it was easy. He travelled to Ireland and arranged for some core samples to be taken, but he forged the reports using Clandillon's logo from their website and convinced Deri that there were good prospects. Then he told Deri that he would look after the acquisition of the lands so that they could stake a claim and start exploration.

"And when were you going to cash in and skip?" Hays said.

"I needed to sell a few more parcels to Chuck. It was easy money, and he was willing to pay a lot of dollars for free access to the land. I guess I would have hung around till all that was done if it wasn't for that little minx, Mary. Bitch!"

"Now that's no way to talk about one of my officers, Mr Gilbert. You should have more respect. So, it was greed that was driving you, is that what you're saying?"

"More like taking candy from a baby. But yeah, there was definitely more cash to come – quite a bit more."

"Right. Well, you won't be seeing any of that money now, Mr Gilbert."

"You can't touch that, it's tidied away overseas. Only I can withdraw it, so you can forget that."

"Don't be naïve, Mr Gilbert. You should know that we've already been in touch with the FBI over this whole mess. They have told us that they will have no trouble sequestrating your ill-gotten gains. You're not only friendless – you're broke!"

Hays let the news sink in for a few moments before continuing.

"I think I need an attorney," Gilbert said eventually.

"I do too. But you can't afford one, and I wouldn't rely on one of our duty solicitors if I were you – they're not up to much. Would you like me to ask Mr Deri if he will provide you with a lawyer?" Hays said with a smirk.

Gilbert just grunted.

"OK. Now it's time to tell me about your interaction with the Fahertys. When did you come in contact with them first?"

"That was about eight months ago. I was going around talking to people who were working bits of that common land. Christ! It was like something out of the Great Depression. Old-timers with no machinery trying to scratch a living from bog and rocks. Pathetic. Laughlin Faherty seemed to be doing a bit better. I called to their place a few times and finally found them both there and I put a proposition to them to buy out their interests. The older one, Laughlin, was all in favour. He's had enough of the toil and the bad weather working that useless land. But Davin was all sanctimonious. He couldn't contemplate parting with the land that his father and grandfather had worked all those years. Idiot!"

"Did you try to persuade him?"

"Of course. I gave them money – a sort of advance on the deal. I tried everything, but Davin wouldn't budge. Maybe he thought he could get a massive price for the old place by holding out. I don't know how his mind was working."

"So, you decided you'd see him off, is that it?" Hays said.

"No – no way! I never touched the guy. You can't pin that on me. Whatever happened to him was not of my doing. You have to believe me."

"Wrong again, Mr Gilbert, I don't. From where I'm sitting you had motive and opportunity, and we'll find out about the means in due course. Speaking of which, how did you acquire the Rohypnol that you used on Garda Fallon?"

"I got it on the internet. It's freely available if you know where to look."

"And I imagine arsenic is much the same."

"I wouldn't know, Superintendent."

"Well, it won't be hard for us to discover exactly what you've been buying online anyway. Your computer will hold a history that we can recover no matter how clever you think you have been."

"That's good, because it will prove to you that I didn't buy any arsenic, won't it?"

"Maybe, maybe not. We'll see. I'm going to leave you to think things over now, Mr Gilbert. I'll be back in a while and we'll see what else we're going to charge you with. I need to talk some more with Mr Deri too – find out what he has to say."

"Hmph. I bet he's acting all innocent like he didn't know anything about what was going on. Ask him about the money he gave me to bribe the local officialdom here. See if that gets a reaction!"

Chapter Thirty-three

While Hays had been squeezing Gilbert for information, Laughlin Faherty arrived at Mill Street accompanied by Mary Fallon from Roundstone and Jim Dolan from Clifden. Lyons went downstairs to meet the three of them and called Mary aside.

"Did he say anything on the way in the car, Mary?"

"No. Not a word. But I got the impression he was sort of expecting us at the farm. He was very compliant."

"OK. Thanks. What are your plans now? Are you going straight back out to Roundstone?"

"I thought I might stay in the city overnight, do some late-night shopping, and then get the bus out to Roundstone in the morning. Do you think that would be OK?"

"Of course. It's almost knocking-off time now anyway. If you like we could meet up later and have some food. We can give you a bed for the night if you like too. Save your pennies for the shops."

"That's too much, Inspector. I'll be fine. I'll get a B&B here in the city. It won't cost much at this time of the year."

"Don't be daft, girl. Ours is cheaper and probably cleaner too. Why don't you come back here when you're all shopped out and we'll get a meal and take you home? It's no trouble, honestly."

"Well, if you're sure. That's very kind of you. Will the Superintendent not mind?"

"Leave him to me, Mary. He's a pussycat really!"

* * *

Lyons collected Sally Fahy and they went downstairs to the interview room where Laughlin Faherty was being kept. He looked quite dejected as he sat there in his working clothes, staring at the floor.

When Lyons had set up the tape recorder and said all the usual stuff about who was present and what day and time it was, she turned to Faherty.

"Now, Laughlin. Do you know why you are here?"

"Not really. I suppose it's to do with the drugs."

"It's not, actually. We want to talk to you about Davin's death. Why don't you tell us what you know?"

"You've no idea how hard it is," Faherty said.

"How hard what is, Laughlin?"

"Working that place. The land is so poor. And the weather is usually dreadful. I have to get up at six o'clock every day and go out in the howling wind and the lashing rain to feed the animals. Then I have to look after the house – there's always something needs fixing, and it's a constant battle for money. Bills, bills, all the time. And no help from anyone."

"I can imagine. Not an easy life. So why haven't you sold up?" Fahy said.

"I wanted to. Yer man from the mining company was offering good money. I could sell the animals and get a nice dry cottage or apartment in Clifden and just work as a handyman around the town. That would have done me nicely, but Davin wouldn't hear of it. 'It's our land, Laughlin. It's our heritage – our birthright – just imagine what our father would say if we let it go,' he'd say. I told him that our father didn't have to get up every day and face what I have to deal with. And I told him he was a useless prick."

"What did he think of that?" Lyons said.

"He said that he worked with his brain, not his brawn. He said he could make more money in a week than the farm could earn in a month, and I guess he did help out occasionally with the expenses. But he kept most of it."

"Did you know where his money was coming from?"

"You've seen our place, Sergeant. You know how hard it would be to keep secrets in that house. I could hear him on the phone to his druggie mates – fixing up things, arranging drops and so on."

"And did it never occur to you to report this to the Gardaí?" Fahy said.

"Ah, for fuck sake, don't be so thick!"

Lyons took over.

"What happened then, Laughlin? You may as well know we found the rat poison in your barn, and we've matched it to the substance found in Davin's system after he died."

"You've no idea how lonely I get out there. The place is like a prison. No one to talk to except a few sheep. It fair does my head in sometimes. And then along comes some guy offering to pay us real money to get free of the place, and Davin won't hear of it. Starts calling me names – abusing me."

"How did you administer the poison?"

"That was easy. Vodka. I mixed it up with his drink. I waited till he had had a good few beers so he wouldn't taste it, and then left the vodka bottle beside his bed. I knew he couldn't resist. He drank the lot. Then I wrapped him in the black plastic and put him in the jeep and dumped him away out there at Shannalecka. I didn't think anyone would ever find him. It was damn bad luck."

"What did you plan to do then?" Fahy said.

"I was going to wait a few weeks and contact that American guy again. He used to stay at that fancy hotel in Clifden. I was planning to bite his hand off."

"Do you not think he would have wanted Davin's signature on the paperwork?"

"That's the funny thing. The place is in my name. It's only my father's dying wish that we should own it equally that has the pair of us still there. I'm able to do the deal without Davin but I could never get away with it while he was alive."

Laughlin Faherty continued with his sad story for another half an hour. His confession more or less wrapped up the murder enquiry, but the two Gardaí couldn't help but feel a little sorry for him. Lumbered with a useless sibling, and tied to an impossible situation thanks to his father's dying wishes, Laughlin's mental state had slowly deteriorated until he was driven to commit fratricide. He saw it as the only way out of his desperate situation.

* * *

Lyons brought Laughlin Faherty out to the desk sergeant at Mill Street and he was formally charged with murder. It was too late to get him before a judge that evening, so he was returned to the cells to spend the night.

"Are we going to oppose bail?" Sally Fahy said to Lyons.

"I'll check with Mick, but I doubt it. He needs to get back out to Boolagare to tend to his animals, and while he's awaiting trial, he can get the place ready for mothballing while he's inside, or put it on the market – whatever."

"How long will he get, do you think?" Fahy asked.

"We'll get him psychologically assessed. He might get away with diminished responsibility – so perhaps six to eight years. He could be out in four."

"It's not much for a life, is it?"

"No, but when you take everything into account, he was already serving a life sentence."

* * *

"Hi, Mick. Listen, Mary Fallon is in town. She came in with Laughlin Faherty. I've asked her to stay with us tonight. Is that OK?"

"Yeah, of course. Where is she now?"

"Shopping. I said we might get something to eat on the way home too. Do you mind?"

"No, not at all. I believe congratulations are in order in any case. Faherty has confessed to killing his brother."

"Yes, though it's all a bit tragic to be honest. I don't think I'll be celebrating – well, not too much anyway. What about you and the fragrant Mr Gilbert?"

"Bloody chancer! I don't know what we're going to do with him. I'll have a chat with Finbarr in the morning and see what way the land lies. I'm fed up with this whole thing to be honest. It's a right waste of time."

"What you need, sir, is alcohol and the company of two stunningly beautiful junior officers. Meet us in twenty minutes in the car park. I feel a taxi coming on."

"You're not wrong there. Gotcha! See you soon."

* * *

Mary Fallon got back to Mill Street at quarter to eight, laden with several carrier bags from some of the more expensive shops in the city.

"Look at you! Is there anything left in the shops?" Lyons said, helping her to unload.

"A girl has to do her best, Inspector. There's a certain Guard in a Garda station not too far from here that needs to be made aware of my feminine charms," Fallon said, smiling.

"I see. The one and only Pascal Brosnan, no doubt! And now that we're off duty, it's Maureen and the Superintendent is Mick. OK?"

"Ehh... yes, I guess, Maureen."

The three of them set off by taxi for O'Grady's seafood restaurant in Barna.

With the formalities of their various ranks dispensed with, the trio got on well together. They talked very little about the two cases that they were bringing to a conclusion. Hays quizzed Mary Fallon about her back story. He discovered that her father was a solicitor who practiced in Ballinasloe, but Hays promised not to hold that against her. Mary had been a very bright student at school, and had achieved an impressive 560 points in her Leaving Certificate – enough to allow her to go to university and study law, or anything else she chose. But from an early age, she had wanted to join the Gardaí, and much against her father's wishes, she had applied as soon as she reached eighteen.

Mary had excelled during training in Templemore, and was a little bit disappointed to be posted to what was considered in the force to be a backwater in Clifden.

"But you've seen more action there than most Guards see in their entire careers, Mary. Surely you don't still think of it as the back of beyond?" Lyons said.

"Oh, no, not at all. And when they moved me to Roundstone, I was actually very pleased," Fallon said.

"Nothing to do with the presence of one Pascal Brosnan, I presume?"

Mary blushed and said, "We get on really well together – I mean at the work and all."

"Of course, you do realise that any romantic involvement between serving officers is strictly frowned upon," Hays said, smiling and squeezing Maureen Lyons' hand as he looked affectionately at his partner.

"Of course," Fallon replied, and they all laughed heartily.

Chapter Thirty-four

"Well, Mick, what's the story?" Chief Superintendent Finbarr Plunkett said to Hays the following morning. Hays explained the interview with Jed Gilbert the previous day.

"What are you planning to do with him, then?" Plunkett said.

"I'm not sure, sir. I was hoping you might have some good ideas. We have him on the assault charge, of course. That will stick – it's open and shut. But as to the other stuff, well I'm not so sure. There has been criminal activity, but it could be hard to prove exactly where the crimes took place. It's a bit of a minefield."

"Yes, very drole, Mick, very drole."

"Have you had anything from Dublin about them?"

"Of course, but oddly, not exactly what I was expecting. More like fishing than the usual 'hands off' message I normally get when there are high-powered foreigners involved."

"I don't think this lot have too much influence. The embassy didn't want to know about Gilbert anyway, and if Deri had been making a big fuss, we would have heard about it by now. My guess is that both of them have been at it, and they are in damage limitation mode," Hays said.

"Right. Here's what we'll do. Have another chat with Gilbert. Tell him you're willing to let him go if he gives us the names of the officials here that he's been dropping bribes on. Tell him we won't act on it till he's well clear, in case he fears for his safety. Then pack the pair of them off back to the boonies. Will that lassie out in Roundstone kick off if we don't prosecute Gilbert?"

"No, she'll be fine. I'll get Maureen to have a word with her. She's smart – she'll see the bigger picture, as you always say."

"Good. And, of course, you'll probably want to have a chat with your friendly FBI man before they leave our shores. Just saying."

* * *

Before Hays went to have his chat with Gilbert, he asked Maureen to call Mary Fallon and see if she was OK with them dropping the charges against Gilbert.

"That's not a problem, Inspector. I'd feel a bit of a fool giving evidence of how I was so easily taken in by that slimeball in any case. And I'm still getting lots of sympathy from Pascal, so it's not all bad."

"That's great, Mary. Very helpful, thanks."

"And thank you and the Superintendent for a lovely evening last night, and letting me stay over and all. You're very kind."

"Yes, it was a nice evening. We enjoyed it too."

Lyons relayed the conversation to Hays who was pleased to hear that Plunkett's plan could now go ahead. He went and spoke to Gilbert who was almost ecstatic to hear that the assault charge was being dropped. He willingly gave up the names of the people in the local authorities that he had bribed to complete his land dealings, and Hays made a careful note of them.

"We'll book Mr Deri and yourself on the United Airlines flight to Newark for tomorrow then, Mr Gilbert. But I should advise you that you will be placed on a watch list at our airports, so I would advise you not to turn up here again for a good few years."

"Understood, Superintendent. And thanks for your understanding."

By the time all the formalities were complete, it was early afternoon. Hays was back in his office, and called Agent O'Halloran in the FBI.

"Hi, Ethan, it's Mick Hays here from Galway. Good morning."

"Hi, Mick. What's the story?"

"We're sending Mr Deri and Mr Gilbert back to the States tomorrow morning on the Shannon to Newark flight. I think it gets in at around 3:00 p.m. local time. We haven't charged them with anything, but they have definitely been up to no good – and that goes for both of them. Have you any news from there?"

"Yes, we have. Our local office in Logan unearthed a whistle-blower. He had a few small motoring violations, and the locals were able to persuade him to tell us what he knew about Derivest in exchange for a let off. He has worked for Derivest for several years and had a lot of dirt to reveal about dodgy dealings over land rights and pollution. I think we will arrange to meet our two friends in Newark and treat them to our special brand of hospitality for a few days."

"Excellent. That's great, Ethan. And if you're ever passing this way, or if you need anything else to help convict those two, just give me a call. We'll be glad to help."

"Thanks, Mick. Same goes for you. Bye."

* * *

The two Americans were driven to Shannon the following day. The Garda escort stayed with them until they disappeared down the jetway into the plane, and stayed on to see the aircraft lift off on its way to New Jersey. Neither man had any idea that the FBI would be waiting to greet them on arrival – they were just greatly relieved to be getting away from Ireland where things had gone so badly wrong for them.

Laughlin Faherty was brought before a judge on the same day, accused of the unlawful killing of his brother, Davin. His solicitor, a young, enthusiastic man who had been appointed by the Gardaí to look after Laughlin's interests, asked the judge for bail, and as the Gardaí didn't make any objection, Laughlin was released on bail with the condition that he report to Clifden Garda station once weekly on a day to be agreed between Sergeant Mulholland and himself before the week was out. The judge ordered a psychological assessment to be arranged for him as well, on the prompting of the solicitor.

Lyons, the case now complete for the moment, decided to drive Laughlin Faherty back home herself, and to take the opportunity to call in on Séan Mulholland and the Roundstone Garda station as she was out in that direction.

Faherty made no conversation on the drive which took nearly an hour to accomplish, so Lyons played RTE radio for the journey which absorbed the silence nicely. When she eventually turned into Faherty's yard, she was taken by the depressing nature of the bleak, damp concrete yard, the barn that needed painting, and the little house that looked as if it belonged in the nineteenth century.

"What will you do with the place now, Laughlin?" she asked as the two of them stood in the yard.

"I've been thinking about that. Dinny from over yonder will look after the fields for me in exchange for a bit of grazing. I'll just lock up the house and leave it while I'm away, and then we'll see."

"You wouldn't be tempted to sell up then?" Lyons said.

"Ah, no, Inspector. I've learned my lesson on that score. My father and my brother would come back to haunt me now if I did that. I'll keep it going as long as I'm able."

Lyons left the man to his musings, and drove on into Clifden.

"Ah, Maureen, 'tis yourself," Séan Mulholland said rather unnecessarily when she entered the Garda station. "I'm just putting on the kettle. Will you have a cup?"

"Thanks, Séan. I've just been delivering Laughlin Faherty back to his farm, if you could call it that. God, that place is miserable."

"Like many others out that way. Sure, there's no money to do the places up or anything. The land will never be any good. But the tourists are building nicely. We've had a good year here in the town. And we have the Arts Festival to come yet."

As Mulholland prepared the tea and retrieved a fresh packet of chocolate Goldgrain from the cupboard, Lyons filled him in on the saga of Derivest and the mineral exploration.

"Ah, 'tis just as well, Maureen. Sure, it would have been fierce disruptive if it had gone ahead. You'd have to be giving me a whole new squad to deal with the miners – not to mention the locals with their new-found wealth. We're better off as we are, don't you think?"

Lyons recognised the rhetorical question and said nothing, helping herself to a biscuit and Mulholland's hot mug of strong tea.

"Oh, wait till I tell you, Maureen. You know that lad Ian Callaghan we were after for possibly stabbing Laughlin Faherty? Well, he was only stopped doing about a hundred miles an hour up in Donegal, on his way to the North. The lads recognised him from the information we had circulated."

"Wow, nice one. What's happening to him?"

"Apparently, Inspector O'Higgins is dealing with him. He reckons the young lad will give up some information about the gang that were running the grow house if he's faced with an attempted murder charge," Mulholland said.

"Excellent."

Epilogue

Laughlin Faherty faced his trial stoically. The psychological assessment had shown that his circumstances, and the behaviour of his younger sibling, had definitely had some influence on his actions. The judge was sympathetic to the defendant, and at the end of the three days, sentenced Laughlin to seven years in custody, the last year of which was suspended.

Laughlin served his time in Castlerea. He was very well behaved, and managed to keep himself largely to himself, but he used the time to achieve a number of City & Guilds qualifications in plumbing, decorating, woodwork, bricklaying and welding. He accumulated various other qualifications that would allow him to offer his services as more than a handyman when he got out, and he figured that with the extra income that this work would provide, together with the money from the farm, he would be able to sustain himself and make improvements to his house and lands.

He was released after serving four and a half years, and was pleased to find that his cottage in Boolagare had survived as well as he had while he was away. Yes, it was musty and a bit mouldy in places, but the structure was sound and it didn't take him long to spruce the place up using his newly acquired talents. He converted Davin's end of the house into a comfortable sitting room, installed a new kitchen, replaced the old, draughty windows all around, and put in a new Stanley range that was connected to central heating radiators in each room. He insulated the roof, and by the time he was finished, the place looked totally refreshed and was much more habitable.

At first, some of the locals were reluctant to employ him, but others gave him a chance, and within a year he found his diary full of jobs doing repairs and improving many of the houses and commercial properties in the area. It wasn't long before he settled into a productive and enjoyable life where he had plenty of everything that a man needs.

Two years after he was released from jail, he was doing up a shop in Letterfrack when he became friendly with one of the shop girls. They were both shy, but somehow managed to strike up a relationship, and a year later they were married. Two years after that, his new wife produced twins, one boy and one girl, and Laughlin finally had a son and heir to pass the family farm onto. His father could finally rest easy in his grave.

The Americans didn't fare so well. The FBI arrested them both when they arrived back to Newark. They had built a strong case against both of the men, and prosecuted it enthusiastically. Derivest had to close, and as the FBI investigated more of its activities, much wrongdoing was uncovered. It transpired that Chuck Deri had known more or less everything about Jed Gilbert and his activities, save for the forged soil analysis reports. He had been duped, and got his revenge by telling the FBI all about Gilbert's malfeasance.

By the time the FBI were finished with them, they both got long prison sentences.

Out in Connemara, when the word got back to the community that the mining adventure had all been some kind of ghastly hoax, a committee was formed to see if the lands could be wrested free of the new owners. It took several years, most of which was consumed by legal arguments that spanned almost the entire globe, but eventually the Supreme Court in Ireland ruled that, as virtually all of the transactions involving the transfer of ownership of the land in question had been fraudulent, it should be returned to prior ownership – namely that it should revert to being common land. Laughlin Faherty had been an active member of the committee, which helped greatly with his rehabilitation in the community in which he lived.

Character List

Sergeant Séan Mulholland – an experienced Garda Sergeant who runs the Garda station in Clifden in his own, somewhat old-fashioned way.

Jim Dolan – an astute Garda who works with Sergeant Mulholland in Clifden.

Séamus Gill – another Garda based in the Clifden station.

Bridget O'Toole – the postmistress from Clifden who knows a great deal about everyone from the town.

Aoife O'Toole – Bridget O'Toole's daughter.

Davin Faherty – one of two brothers that occupy an old homestead at Boolagare. Davin doesn't like hard physical work, so he leaves that side of things to his elder brother.

Laughlin Faherty – toils night and day to scratch a living from the poor land that has been handed down to him by his father and grandfather.

Paddy the postman – reliably delivers the mail all along the route from Galway to Clifden every weekday.

Maureen Lyons – now a Senior Inspector, assigned to the newly formed Serious and Organised Crime Unit (SOCU) in Galway.

Mick Hays – Superintendent in overall charge of Garda operations in Galway and life partner of Maureen Lyons.

Finbarr Plunkett – the Chief Superintendent in Galway, a wily and experienced senior officer who knows how to navigate the often tricky politics of the job.

Peadar Tobin – a Garda who has been seconded to the SOCU and used to work with Sergeant Mulholland in Clifden.

Eamon Flynn – an inspector with the Gardaí who runs the main detective unit in Galway.

Pascal Brosnan – a good-looking young Garda who is in charge of the station in Roundstone.

Mary Fallon – Pascal's assistant who thinks a great deal of her colleague.

Tadgh Deasy – a somewhat dodgy car dealer from close to Roundstone who helps the police out on occasion.

Sally Fahy – a Detective Sergeant seconded to the SOCU when it was being set up.

Nikola – a pretty Polish girl who works as a receptionist in the Alcock and Brown hotel in Clifden.

Jed Gilbert – an American mining expert with a few interesting side-lines.

Chuck Deri – the proprietor of Derivest Mining Corporation, a mining company based in Logan, Utah.

Liam O'Higgins – an Inspector with the Drugs Squad in Galway.

James McMahon – an architect who has proven to be very useful to the Galway Gardaí on a number of occasions.

Festus Greeley – an old-timer that has a smallholding near Shannalecka.

Sinéad Loughran – a forensic scientist with a great sense of humour.

Dr Julian Dodd – the pathologist attached to the Galway Gardaí.

Anselm O'Shaughnessy – a solicitor.

Ethan O'Halloran – an FBI agent whose ancestors come from Ireland.

Ian Callaghan – a young man who finds it easy to attract trouble.

Malcolm Clandillon – runs a geological analysis company in the United Kingdom.

Judge Meehan – presides over the Galway District Court.

If you enjoyed this book, please let others know by leaving a quick review on Amazon. Also, if you spot anything untoward in the paperback, get in touch. We strive for the best quality and appreciate reader feedback.

editor@thebookfolks.com

www.thebookfolks.com

BOOKS BY DAVID PEARSON

In this series:

Murder on the Old Bog Road (Book 1)
Murder at the Old Cottage (Book 2)
Murder on the West Coast (Book 3)
Murder at the Pony Show (Book 4)
Murder on Pay Day (Book 5)
Murder in the Air (Book 6)
Murder at the Holiday Home (Book 7)
Murder on the Peninsula (Book 8)
Murder at the Races (Book 9)
Murder in a Safe Haven (Book 10)
Murder in an Irish Bog (Book 11)

In the Dublin Homicides series:

A Deadly Dividend
A Fatal Liaison
The China Chapter
Lethal in Small Doses

THE DUBLIN HOMICIDES SERIES:

Two very different police officers work together to solve cases in this mystery series with a cozy feel.

For Detective Inspector Aidan Burke, policing Dublin's streets is a duty, but protecting his officers comes first. That provides a good environment for promising detectives like DS Fiona Moore to grow. As this series of murder mysteries set in the metropolitan but at times parochial city and its surroundings progresses, we see Moore tackle difficult and dangerous cases with a good success rate. As Burke himself rises in rank, they become a formidable crime fighting duo.

All four books are free with Kindle Unlimited and available in paperback.

Made in the USA
Monee, IL
14 May 2021

68688250R00134